CW01333145

The Waif's Lost Family

IRIS COLE

VIDORRA HOUSE

©Copyright 2023 Iris Cole

All Rights Reserved

License Notes

This Book is licensed for personal enjoyment only. It may not be resold. No part of this work may be reproduced in any form or by any electronic or mechanical means including information storage and retrieval systems, without written permission from the author.

Disclaimer

This story is a work of fiction, any resemblance to people is purely coincidence. All places, names, events, businesses, etc. are used in a fictional manner. All characters are from the imagination of the author.

Would you like a free book?

[CLAIM](#)

[THE FOUNDLING BABY](#)

[HERE](#)

Table of Contents

Would you like a free book? iv

PART ONE 2

   Chapter One 3

   Chapter Two 35

   Chapter Three 63

   Chapter Four 83

Part Two 107

   Chapter Five 108

   Chapter Six 131

   Chapter Seven 155

Part Three 183

   Chapter Eight 185

   Chapter Nine 209

Part Four 249

   Chapter Ten 251

   Chapter Eleven 273

   Chapter Twelve 293

   Epilogue 321

Preview 329

THE STONEPICKERS CHRISTMAS PROMISE 331
    Chapter One 333
    Chapter Two 345

PART ONE

Chapter One

The cotton mill echoed with cacophonous sound, but none of it came from the toiling figures of the men, women and children who laboured within its dark and dusty belly. Everything in the mill seemed to be contributing to the din except for them: the roaring steam engine that drove the machines, the hiss of yarn spinning on the billies, the clatter and thump of the mule, the clack and judder of the looms. Among the chaos of noise, the people working inside seemed like insignificant ants, crawling miserably across the face of the heartless industry. And above everything hung a pall of dust, barely broken by the bits of light that came in through the high windows, fading rapidly as the sun began to set and ineffectively replaced by dusty gas lamps that burned like fevered eyes in the choking darkness.

Gwen Hopewell knew very well why everyone inside the cotton mill was so utterly silent. There was neither time, nor breath, nor energy left for talking. Everyone in the mill was toiling just as hard as she was, even her little sister, Roberta. It hardly seemed fair that Roberta should be here beside her, hastening up and down the length of the billy as what seemed like a hundred lengths of white yarn spun upon it. She was only ten years old, and her pale little face was already pinched with exhaustion, even though it was only six o' clock; there were still hours of work waiting for them. Roberta's blue eyes were bloodshot as they scanned up and down the rows of threads, searching for any imperfection.

There was so much that Gwen wanted to do for Roberta. She wanted to give her a word of encouragement, or to help her somehow, or even just to stop and wrap her in an embrace, as if that would do her aching little body any good. But Gwen was only twelve herself, and there was no time to stop, no breath to speak. Dust had been choking her lungs all day, and she kept wiping her nose on a tattered sleeve as she hurried up and down her end of the billy, waiting for a thread to snap.

It was impossible to hear the yarn when it broke. Everything was just too loud. But Gwen's eyes, strained as they were by a full day of keeping her gaze locked steadily on the yarn, instantly picked out the flying end of a broken piece. She broke into a jog, hurrying to grab the broken end. The wheel was spinning frantically; machinery clicked and snapped dangerously under her fingers like a rabid dog. Her fingers were aching from the work, and the yarn burned her skin, but she found the other end and tied it in a brisk, quick movement.

The yarn sprung tight in her hands, and Gwen let go, stepping back. The billy went on working, the yarn went on spinning, and Gwen allowed herself a short breath of relief.

"Gwen?"

Roberta's voice sounded quiet, but Gwen knew she was shouting at the top of her voice just to make herself heard. She turned, forcing a smile for her sister's sake. "What is it?" she yelled.

Roberta dragged a filthy hand over her brow, smearing sweat and dirt together. "I'm thirsty," she shouted.

Gwen's heart felt like it was being trampled. "We'll get a water break soon," she bellowed back. Roberta gave her the long, silent look of a child who knew she was being lied to.

There were so few water breaks, and the air was so dry...

Then Gwen saw it: the white end of a broken piece of yarn, flapping hopelessly on the far side of the billy, where Roberta was supposed to be watching it.

"Bobbie!" she gasped, more terrified than exasperated. She shoved past her sister and ran to the broken thread, but her hands were already sweaty with fear. The yarn slipped through her fingers, burning her skin, and she had to grab at it twice before she could finally tie it off –

"OI!" thundered a masculine voice. "YOU!"

Gwen whipped around. A heavyset man with a week's greasy beard was lumbering among the machinery towards her, a grubby cigarette dangling from the corner of his mouth. That cigarette seemed to be permanently part of him; its cheap smoke had long since stained his dirty, overlong fingernails a nasty shade of yellow, which matched his jaundiced eyes as they fixed upon Gwen.

Her heart thudded painfully in her chest. Wherever their supervisor went, people dropped their eyes to the ground, their shoulders hunching in simple fear.

Hugh Worley leaned on a walking stick as he came up to Gwen, still sucking on the ever-present cigarette. It wobbled in his mouth as he spoke.

"What's the matter with you?" he snarled, his lips flapping loose and fleshy over each syllable. "You let that thread stay broken for far too long." He lifted the stick and held it across his body, slapping it into his free palm with a meaty thud.

Gwen knew the feel of that walking stick, and she couldn't take her eyes off it. Behind her, she could hear Roberta whimpering with fear. A flare of anger rose in her. She wasn't the one who had been neglecting her threads.

"This is your fault," she muttered.

"What was that?" shouted Worley, leaning a little closer so that his sweaty, smoky odour could be added to the general stench of the cotton mill.

Gwen took a deep breath. As always, she knew what she had to do.

"It was my fault, sir!" she shouted. "I wasn't looking!"

A dangerous gleam filled Worley's small, angry eyes. He raised the stick. "Hold out your hand," he ordered.

Gwen's eyes prickled with tears. At least the beating was better than having her wages docked. She did so, holding out her left hand, and screwed her eyes tightly shut.

"Now don't move," snapped Worley.

Gwen didn't dare. To flinch away was to incur an extra blow. There was a whistling sound, and the stick thumped down across Gwen's palm with a burning pain. She forced herself to stay still, keeping her flinches to her shoulders and hips as the stick thumped home over and over again until her palm went from stinging to burning to aching to numb.

Worley was out of breath when he stopped. Sweat dribbled down his filthy face as he glared at her. "Now get back to work," he spat. "Don't make me take away your wages."

"Yes, sir. I will, sir," Gwen gasped through her tears.

Worley strode away, and Gwen turned back to her work, letting the tears fall unchecked down her cheeks. She felt a fluttering touch on her arm and glanced down to see Roberta looking up at her, her eyes brimming with tears.

"I'm so sorry," Roberta said.

Gwen turned away. "I'm not angry," she said, and it was the truth. "Let's just get back to work."

Work: ultimately, that was all that their lives had become.

~ ~ ~ ~ ~

There had been a slightly better time once, but Gwen never spoke of it. She didn't want Roberta to know that their lives used to be better. She didn't want Roberta to grieve a better life the way she was doing right now.

The walk home was not a long one, but for Gwen, it was always the most miserable part of her day. It was very dark by the time they left the ugly, looming building of the cotton mill behind and turned their steps towards the housing – if it could be called that – that gave mill workers somewhere to live in the nearby suburbs. At least in the early mornings, Gwen had a little strength, even if it was very dark. But now, her legs were trembling from exhaustion, her feet aching steadily. And there was a throbbing pain in her palm from the beating it had taken by Worley.

Keeping Roberta's small hand firmly clutched in her uninjured hand, Gwen tried to think of something else as she walked back towards home. Sometimes, like today, her mind wandered unchecked back to that other time. They had lived in a tenement then too, but at least they hadn't shared it with another family. In fact, they'd had two sleeping pallets: one for her and Roberta, and another one for Mama and Papa. Food had been scarce, but they never went a day without eating. And there had been laughter in their home at times.

That had all been before Papa died trying to save a little scavenger from under one of the cotton mill's cruel machines. He had barely been buried when

Gwen, only six at the time, was sent to work in the very same mill.

She pushed the thoughts aside and forced a smile for Roberta. "Nearly home, love," she said, giving her sister a little tug to encourage her to keep up.

"My feet are so tired," Roberta complained.

"I know. I know." Gwen sighed. "But it's not far. Come on now."

She tried to keep her eyes straight forward as they entered the slum. All around them, a scene of utter despair and squalor rolled past, every block worse than the one preceding it. Row after row of houses with thin walls, broken windows and rattling roofs watched them pass like silent beggars ignored on street corners, their fading paint and empty window-frames crying out silently for help and attention. The paving had long since given way to mud, which sucked at Gwen's tired feet and seeped through the gaps in her shoes so that her socks turned slowly cold and sticky.

Around her, a drove of people, faceless, voiceless, the very life sucked out of them by their day at the mill, were journeying towards their insufficient homes and meagre suppers just as she was. Their faces were hidden by the darkness, broken only intermittently by old streetlamps lit with flickering, sickly flames.

All of the people moved with the same broken desperation as Gwen did; driven home only by the knowledge that there might be rest there, their toiling, aching bodies barely capable of the final effort of walking home. Yet even these were better off than the few figures that Gwen saw huddled in nooks and crannies, alleyways and odd corners. She tried her best not to look at them, but sometimes the horrors dragged her eyes unbidden from her path. An old woman, lying on her side, stretched out on the mud, looking stone dead except for the odd breath that lifted her old chest and stirred the lock of muddy grey hair hanging over her face.

A young man, leaning against the wall of an alley, staring down at the hem of his tattered shirt, pulling off bits of thread that were fraying loose and tucking them carefully into his pocket as if there was some use left in them. A young woman lay curled beside him, a baby in her arms. The baby was crying, a thin, weak, monotonous wail; the woman did not wake, and the man did not spare it a second glance.

As Gwen passed by, she saw that the woman had a suppurating wound on her elbow where it pressed into the filthy street.

She shuddered, tucking an arm around Roberta's shoulders and turning her away so that she wouldn't see the horrifying sight. "Nearly home, Bobbie," she said, trying to make her voice as cheerful as possible. "Tomorrow's Sunday, too, so we don't have to go to work. And I'm sure there's still a little piece of that salt fish for dinner. You and Teddy can share it."

Roberta cheered up a little. "Yes, there is!" she said. "But why should Teddy have any? He's just been sitting at home all day." She frowned. "And he's six years old already. He should be working, just like I was, at his age."

Gwen knew, because it was the same age that she, too, had been sent to the cotton mill when their father had died. Being a scavenger — crawling under those great, clanking, deadly machines to clean them while they were running — was dangerous and horrible work, but nothing could ever be more horrible than watching her tiny sister do it. There had been times when Roberta had cried through an entire sixteen-hour shift, the tears washing twin trails of clean skin through the grubbiness of her face.

Yet even that could never be worse than what had happened to Joey.

"You know why Mama won't send him to the cotton mill, Bobbie," said Gwen, dragging her mind away from the awful memory; the blood, the screams... and then the silence.

"But she sent us," said Roberta.

"That was before Joey," said Gwen.

Silence fell between them, the way it always did any time Joey's name was mentioned. Roberta gave Gwen a sheepish look. "I'm sorry," she said. "I didn't mean..."

"I know," said Gwen.

"I'm just hungry. And I think Teddy should be pulling his weight some way or another."

"Never mind that now," said Gwen. "Look — we're home."

They turned left into the doorway of one of the many buildings that all looked the same. Roberta pushed the door open as Gwen cast a glance up to the third window on the right, their window. It was boarded up, and there was no sound from inside.

They walked into a dinghy hallway and followed a set of stairs that crackled ominously under their feet until they reached the third floor and their tenement. Gwen laid a hand on the door; there was no knob or latch, just a piece of worn string that hooked around a nail. She took a deep breath, trying to steel herself for another evening at home, and pushed the door open.

The interior was a mess of hopeless squalor. With the window boarded up, only chinks of light from the streetlamp outside could even hope to enter the room.

After the vastness of the cotton mill, the room was puny – but its atmosphere no less stifling, thick with the odour of unwashed humanity. A single candle guttered on an upturned bucket on the floor. Together with the light from measly fire that spluttered miserably in the single hearth, the candle illuminated the small room, which served as two family homes.

Nearest to the door, there were two sleeping pallets; one contained a tousle-haired mass of hungry, bony children, who slept the sleep of the sick under a piece of sacking for a blanket. Their mother perched on the edge of the pallet beside them. On the other pallet, an enormous, hairy, shirtless man lay supine, his bearded chin pointing towards the roof, the tangle of his chest hair no less dark and meaningless than the mass of lines on his forehead. His eyes were closed, but his wife watched him as though he might explode at any moment.

Gwen knew why. Mr. Brown had a nasty temper when he had been drinking, and he had always been drinking. She could smell the stale reek of old alcohol rolling off his breath as he slept, and she tiptoed across the floor, avoiding Mrs. Brown's eyes.

Stepping around Mr. Brown's disgustingly hairy bare feet, Gwen reached for the thin, grubby curtain that separated her home from the Brown's'. She held it aside as Roberta slipped through the gap, then followed it into the tiny area that the Hopewell family called home. Here, there was no hearth, and just a single narrow sleeping pallet pushed up against the wall.

There was about four square feet of floor space in all, and Gwen's little brother was sitting on it, playing contentedly with a broken matchstick and a piece of string. He dropped them both as he looked up, and his dirty little face lit up. "Gwen! Bobbie!" he whispered, hurrying over to them and throwing his arms around Gwen's knees.

Gwen felt everything inside her melting. She crouched down and wrapped her arms around Teddy. "Hello, love," she whispered.

"Hush," said a reedy voice from the sleeping pallet. "Mr. Brown is asleep."

Gwen looked up. Her mother, bone-thin, sat on the pallet, a half-finished slop-shop jacket draped across her knees. She was sewing it with trembling fingers, not looking up from her work when Roberta and Gwen came in. Her legs were stretched out on the pallet, bare feet exposed beneath her fraying skirt. Even though it had been years since Mama had last worked in the factory, Gwen was still always startled by the sight of her legs.

Even though Mama's feet lay several inches apart on the pallet, her shins tapered sharply towards one another. Under her skirt, Gwen knew that Mama's knees were touching. They had given in after decades of standing in the cotton mill and not eating enough. Like Gwen, Mama had started as a scavenger when she was only six.

The mill had taken everything from her, even Joey. Gwen reminded herself of this when Mama's tone scalded her weary heart.

"Don't worry, Mama." She forced a smile. "We'll be very quiet."

"Very quiet," echoed Teddy, turning his great, blue eyes up towards Gwen.

She smiled down at him, more easily this time. "I brought some bread for supper," she said. "And there's salt fish for you and Bobbie, Teddy."

At this, Mama finally set aside her work and looked up. "Isn't there enough for you to have some too, Gwen?" she asked.

"Oh, no thank you, Mama," said Gwen. "I don't need it."

Mama's eyes dwelt on her for a long moment, softening. "Come here, love," she said, holding out an arm. "Bobbie, get the bread – we'll eat together."

Gwen went eagerly to her mother's side. She sat down on the pallet, feeling the hard wooden slats on her thighs, and Mama pulled her into a gentle embrace.

"My children, my children," she sighed. "What in this world would I do without you?"

Gwen buried her face in Mama's neck. "You don't have to be without us, Mama," she said. "I promise."

Mama hugged her tighter, trembling. Gwen knew she was thinking of Joey.

The screams filled her mind again, and she pushed them away. She could never let that happen to her family again.

~ ~ ~ ~ ~

Sunday flitted by much too quickly. It was spent the way Gwen and Roberta spent nearly every Sunday; curled upside by side on the sleeping pallet, finally claiming the sleep that their bodies had been craving all week long. Besides, if they slept through most of the day, then they wouldn't realize how hungry they were. Occasionally, Gwen had half woken to hear Teddy playing too loudly or asking Mama when there would be something to eat again, but Mama would always hush him quickly, and Gwen could drift back to sleep.

By contrast, as usual, Monday's shift at the mill seemed a thousand hours long. Gwen's hand still ached from the beating it had taken from Worley, and piecing was a constant battle. At least this time, Roberta had kept her eyes on her threads, not letting them break on her watch like she had done on Saturday.

Still, Gwen felt as exhausted as though she had never had a day off in the six years since she had started working at the cotton mill. She plodded up the wobbly stairs of their tenement with her head held low, interested only in food and sleep. Roberta was close on her heels, clutching all the food that they could buy with their meagre earnings on a Monday; the rent had been paid that morning, but by tomorrow they would already have to start setting most of their wages aside to pay the rent again the following week.

Tired though she was, the moment Gwen pushed the door open and stepped into the Brown's half of the tenement, she knew instantly that something was terribly amiss.

Mr. Brown wasn't home.

She stared. The room seemed bigger without his presence, yet his absence had failed to abate Mrs. Brown's fear. She was sitting on her pallet, hugging her children to her and weeping, a steady, mournful wail that seemed to be wearing thin from constant crying. Gwen stared at her, then glanced at Roberta, who shrugged. Part of her urged her to reach out and wrap her arms around the young mother and her starving little children, but she did not have the strength.

She turned away instead and pushed through the curtain, and that was where things were even more wrong. Teddy was sitting in a corner, clutching his knees to his chest, his eyes the only clean and white things in the entire tenement; they were very wide and round with fear.

And Mama wasn't working. Unlike Roberta and Gwen, Mama didn't have Sundays; she had to work constantly in order to meet the ridiculous quotas that the slop-shop gave her. Gwen couldn't remember the last time she'd seen her mother doing anything other than working or sleeping or eating, but right now, Mama wasn't doing any of those things. She was just... sitting. Her eyes were wide too, and she was staring into the middle distance, her face utterly ashen under its usual layer of grime.

If Teddy had not been sitting there, alive and well, Gwen would have feared the worst. Mama looked the way she did when Gwen had come home to tell her about...

No! Gwen couldn't allow herself to think Joey's name, not now. "Mama?" she gasped, the word coming out small and trembling.

Mama blinked. She looked up at Gwen, her eyes only half focused. "Children," she croaked, forcing something like a smile.

"What's the matter, Mama?" Roberta went over to her and sat down on the edge of the pallet, a few feet from Mama, as if fearful that she might break her if she touched her. "Is it your legs again?"

"No, no, darling." Mama paused, wrestling with tears. "It's… it's…"

"Please." Gwen fell to her knees on the end of the pallet. "Please, Mama, what's going on?"

"Where's Mr. Brown?" asked Roberta.

"He's left," said Mama.

There was a beat of silence. Gwen didn't understand. "But why does Mrs. Brown look so worried?" she asked. "Normally she's glad when he's gone, even if he comes home so drunk and angry."

"You don't understand, Gwendoline." Mama's tone grew harsh, and she looked up at Gwen with burning eyes. "He's left her. He's gone. He's not coming back. She's going to be on her own now with those little ones…" Her voice broke, and she dropped her gaze to her lap again.

"What will she do?" asked Roberta.

"What we all do, Bobbie." Mama swallowed. "Whatever we have to do, to keep our children safe." She looked up at them again and this time there were tears trembling in her eyes. "I have terrible news."

"What is it?" asked Gwen.

"The rent..." Mama took a shaky breath. "The landlord has raised it. It's one and a half times what it used to be."

"No!" Gwen felt as though she'd just received a kick in the stomach.

"How?" cried Roberta, jumping to her feet. "How could he do that?"

"It's his building," said Mama. "He can do as he pleases."

"But he must know that the mill hasn't increased our wages in years," said Roberta. "How are we to survive, Mama?"

Gwen stared at her mother, desperate for an answer. But the iron resolve that had filled Mama's voice only a moment earlier seemed to be gone now. Her features crumpled, and tears started pouring down her cheeks.

"I don't know, Bobbie," she wept. "I don't know. I just don't know what to do. I don't know what we are going to do."

Gwen felt as though her innards had transformed to ice. She realized that her hands were shaking, and she interlaced her fingers, staring down at them. Mama was shattered. There was nothing left in her, and Roberta was staring at her with tears trickling down her cheeks.

"What are we going to do, Gwen?" asked a soft voice by Gwen's knees.

She looked down. Teddy had gripped her dress in both of his little fists, and he stared up at her, his eyes wide.

"I don't want to be homeless," whispered Roberta, turning to Gwen. "Winter is coming. We'll die out there."

Gwen thought of the homeless people they saw every day as they walked home from work, and everything inside her quailed. She knew they couldn't survive – Mama with her knock knees, tiny Teddy...

There was only one thing she could think of. She bent down and put her hands on Teddy's shoulders. "Teddy, my love," she said, "you'll have to start working."

"No!" Mama's shout was louder than Gwen had expected. She shot to her feet, wobbling on her crooked legs, and seized Teddy as if Gwen had hurt him. Hugging the child to her chest, she stared at Gwen with bloodshot, teary eyes. "My boy won't go to that awful place. He won't. He won't!"

"Mama, would you rather we starved?" cried Gwen. "We're starving as it is."

"I would rather starve than see him die as Joey did," spat Mama.

"I would care for him," said Gwen. "I'd watch him, like I did with Bobbie."

"And like you did with Joey?" Mama snapped.

Gwen took a step back as though she had been physically struck. Sensing her pain, Mama set down Teddy at once, reaching towards Gwen. "Darling, I'm sorry. I didn't mean it. I..."

"No," said Gwen, pulling back from Mama's attempt at an embrace. "You're right. I should have watched Joey." She took a deep breath. "But it's true that we won't survive if we don't get more money, Mama."

"Teddy has to do *something*," said Roberta.

"I will, I will," said Teddy, clutching at Mama's skirt. "I'll help, Mama, let me help."

"But don't send him to the cotton mill," said Gwen, exhaustion and fear tugging at every word. "Let him beg. Look at him. He would be a wonderful beggar."

Mama and Gwen both stared down at Teddy. He gazed back with his guileless blue eyes, set in a pale face surrounded by angelic golden curls.

"You're right," said Mama softly. "Oh, Teddy." She crouched down with an effort, grunting with pain as her faltering knees trembled, and wrapped the child in her arms. "I didn't want to let you go," she whispered. "But I have no choice now. I can't bear for you to leave this tenement every day, but neither can I bear to see you hungry on the streets."

"I'll be all right, Mama," said Teddy, with innocent optimism. "Gwen will show me what to do."

Mama looked up at Gwen with tears standing in her eyes. "Please," she whispered. "Take care of him, Gwen."

Gwen swallowed hard against the ache in her chest. "I promise," she said.

She had made that promise once before. But this time she was even more determined to keep it.

Chapter Two

Gwen could hear Teddy sniffling quietly beside her as they walked out of the slum. She held his little hand tightly, trying not to think of the long day that lay before him. Her shift at the cotton mill was dangerous and hard and awful, but at least she had Roberta with her now. Teddy would spend the day facing the entire city alone.

She tried not to think of what it had been like when she was a scavenger herself, sent to work alone every morning at the same age that Teddy was now. Instead, when they reached the crossroad where they parted ways every morning, she bent down and gave Teddy her best smile.

"All right, Teddy," she said. "Remember to be home by the time they start lighting the streetlamps."

"I will." Teddy swallowed and wiped grubby knuckles over his cheeks, smearing them with dirt and tears.

"Why are you crying, Ted?" asked Gwen, her heart breaking.

"I don't want to get lost again." Teddy's lower lip trembled. "I was so frightened yesterday. I thought I'd never find my way home."

"Don't worry," said Gwen. "You'll find your way." Truth be told, she had no idea how Teddy was managing to navigate the city on her own. "You found your way home yesterday, didn't you?"

"It was so dark by then," Teddy whispered. "Can't Mama come with me?"

"You know she can't, love," said Gwen. "Her legs are too sore. She can hardly walk at all, let alone go across the city with you."

Teddy wiped at his eyes again, nodding and sniffling. Gwen sighed. "Come here." She wrapped her arms around the little boy, feeling his bony little body against her own, and her heart felt like it was being slowly crushed.

"Do I have to go, Gwen?" Teddy whispered.

"You know you do," snapped Roberta. "Otherwise we'll die."

"Bobbie!" Gwen glared at her. "You're not helping."

Roberta's face fell, and she lowered her eyes to the ground. "Sorry," she whispered. "I'm just... I'm just so hungry."

"I know." Gwen sighed, trying to ignore the steady ache in the pit of her own belly. It had been two days since any of them had eaten except for the single rusk she and Roberta were given at work every day; Gwen had kept hers for Mama and Teddy, by a supreme effort of will. "But you're going to bring back some more money tonight, aren't you, Teddy? It's only because of you that we've been able to pay the rent at all for the past two weeks. Maybe you'll get some more today, and then we can have something for supper."

"But why did the landlord make our rent more expensive?" Teddy asked, staring up at her. "Doesn't he know we're going to starve?"

"He just doesn't care, Teddy," said Roberta.

"I'm afraid she's right." Gwen sighed. "There are a lot of people in the world who don't care." She thought of Worley.

"But why?" said Teddy. "The landlord is always wearing nice clothes, and he's so fat. Doesn't he have enough food? Why can't we have enough food, too?"

Teddy's questions were making Gwen's headache. She rested her hands on his shoulders and kissed the top of his head, wishing that he had a hat she could pull down over his frozen little ears. "I don't know, love," she said. "Run along now. We'll see you tonight."

Teddy nodded, dragging a hand under his runny nose. "See you," he mumbled.

Gwen stood up and walked away quickly, grabbing Roberta's hand as she did so. She didn't dare to look back over her shoulder.

She knew that if she did so, she wouldn't be able to tear herself away from her little brother's sad eyes.

~ ~ ~ ~ ~

It had been another long, hard shift. They were all long and hard, of course; but today had been worse than ever. The cotton mill's owners were displeased with its profitability. Worley had told all the workers that some of them would be dismissed, and that anyone who displeased him that day would be subject to instant dismissal.

As a result, everyone had worked at the best speed they could muster. The billies spun faster, the threads came quicker, and more of them snapped, but Gwen didn't dare to look up from them even for a moment, rushing up and down the length of the cotton mule as she hastened to tie off any broken pieces.

Her head, hands, and feet ached uncontrollably as she stumbled up to the door of their tenement, half dragging Roberta along by her hand. She was so, so hungry, and the feeling of her lunch rusk bumping against her thigh where it rested in her skirt pocket was tempting beyond words. But she had to keep it for Mama and Teddy, just in case Teddy's begging had been unsuccessful today.

When she opened the door, however, all thoughts of her hunger fled from her mind. Mama was sitting on Mrs. Brown's sleeping pallet. The Brown children were all huddled in a corner, and Mrs. Brown had her arms around Mama, who was soaking wet and crying with all of her heart. The hopeless sobs reverberated through the tenement just as Mrs. Brown's sobs had a few weeks ago.

"Mama!" Gwen rushed to her, grabbing Mama's arm. "What is the matter? What's happened?"

Mama raised her tear-streaked face to Gwen, seizing her shoulders in hands that trembled with a terrified strength. "Gwendoline, where is your brother?" she cried, her hoarse voice a harpy's shriek of pain.

"Teddy?" Gwen felt her veins fill with ice.

"Where is he?" yelled Mama.

"Isn't he home?" cried Gwen.

"If he was home, would I be weeping?" shouted Mama.

Gwen's heart was thundering, but a part of her cried out at the injustice of it all. She was so tired, so hungry, and so cold, but even the morsel of food and uncomfortable bedding that were her unhappy lot were being denied her now. Outside, a steady sheet of gentle rain had just started falling. Everything inside her trembled at the very thought of turning around and heading back down those stairs.

But Teddy... oh, poor, tiny Teddy, alone in that vast city.

"I'm going to find him, Mama," said Gwen. She straightened up. "Don't worry. I'll find him." She turned to Roberta. "Bobbie, stay here with Mama."

"No." Roberta grabbed Gwen's arm. "I'm not going to let you go out there on your own."

"Please, Bobbie," said Gwen.

"No." Roberta's grip tightened on her arm. "I'm coming with you."

Gwen didn't have the energy to argue, and she felt a surge of gratitude towards her sister. "Thank you," she murmured. "Come on. Let's go."

~ ~ ~ ~ ~

"Teddy!" Gwen shouted, cupping her hands around her mouth. "Teddy! Where are you?"

"Come here, Teddy!" Roberta yelled.

Gwen squinted into the driving rain. It was coming down hard now, blowing directly into her face and eyes as she and Roberta struggled up the street. It felt as though they'd been searching for hours, and indeed, the city had grown completely quiet, with the dead stillness of the small hours of the morning. They were several blocks away from where Teddy was supposed to have been begging, and there was no sign of him now.

There was no sign of anything except the pouring rain. They were walking up to a market square, and all the shops were closed and shuttered, the rain hammering against closed doors like an impatient customer. The streets were empty; the light from the streetlamps seemed to pool and trickle like the rain that rushed down the street.

"It's no use." Roberta turned to Gwen, her eyes wide and red with crying. "We'll never find him in this."

"We have to," said Gwen. Her heart felt squeezed at the thought of poor Teddy alone in this terrible rain. "We don't have a choice, Bobbie." She grabbed her sister's hand. "Come on. Let's search to the end of this square, then go on to the next block."

"But how do you know we're not moving further and further away from him?" said Roberta.

"I don't," said Gwen. Frustration boiled in her, born of hunger and exhaustion. "But what do you want me to do? I don't know where to search. I'm just trying my best."

"Sorry." Roberta hung her head.

Gwen knew she may as well have kicked her sister in the teeth, and Roberta was just as weary and hungry as she was. She hated herself for it, hated herself for talking Mama into letting Teddy go out begging, hated herself for letting Joey die.

Sometimes it felt as though Joey's spectre was following her, determined to force her to make the same mistake again.

She pushed the thought away, turning back to her mission, and went on down the street with Roberta trailing behind her. "Teddy!" she shouted against the howling wind, the rain stinging her eyes and skin. "TEDDY!"

"Wait!" Roberta grabbed Gwen's arm. "What was that?"

Gwen shook her arm free. "I didn't hear anything," she said.

"Shah!" Roberta held up a hand. "Listen."

Gwen listened. The wind howled and the rain hissed... and somewhere, wrapped in the cacophony, was a small and fragile sound that could have been her name.

Gwen's heart flipped over. "Teddy?" she shouted. "Teddy!"

"This way!" said Roberta, tugging at her arm. "It's coming from over here."

Roberta dragged Gwen across the square, hurrying to a nook beside the butchery where garbage cans and bits of old barrels littered the small, dark space. There was a little shelter from the wind here, but a stream of fetid, frigid water ran through it, gushing down into the gutter by the sidewalk. Gwen jumped over the gutter and leaned into the dark little alley. "Teddy?" she cried.

This time, she heard it clearly: her brother's weak and feeble voice. "Gwen!" he croaked.

She stared into the darkness, and then she saw him, or rather, his terrified blue eyes. He had tucked himself in between two of the garbage cans, trying to get out of the wind, but his curls were still bouncing and whipping on his forehead from the wind. They were dark with rain, and his entire body was trembling uncontrollably, his lips deep blue.

"Teddy!" Gwen pushed through the garbage and reached for him. He stretched out his skinny, stick-like arms, and she grabbed him, pulling him into her embrace. "Oh, Teddy. Teddy!" She pressed a hand to the back of his head, holding him close against her neck. "Where were you?"

"I got lost," Teddy croaked.

"It's all right." Roberta clutched Teddy's little hand, then gasped and began to chafe it. "Gwen, he's so cold."

Gwen knew. The tiny body was shaking so powerfully against her own that she was half surprised not to hear his very bones rattle. "We're going to get you home," she said. "We're going to take you straight home, Teddy."

"I'm so hungry," Teddy whispered, leaning his exhausted little head against Gwen's shoulder.

"Do you have some money?" Roberta asked. "I'll get you something – I – I'll find someone open at this time of night." Her voice faltered as she realized the falsehood of her promise.

"No. I don't have anything." Teddy lay limply in Gwen's arms as she carried him out of the alley and into the market square. "A big boy pushed me down and took everything. That's when I got lost. I chased him... I just wanted to help pay for everything." He began to cry. "I just wanted something to eat."

"It's all right," Gwen whispered, hurrying back towards home. "It's all right, Teddy."

But when he wrapped his freezing little hands around her neck, and when she heard the awful rattle in his breathing as he sobbed, she knew that it was very far from all right.

~ ~ ~ ~ ~

Teddy's blue eyes burned with fever. He was staring up at the ceiling, but it was as though he was seeing something completely different; his eyes moved to and fro like he was watching something. There was so much horror in them, and awful shudders ran up and down his spine.

It was strange to see a red flush on his cheeks. Gwen didn't think she could remember a time when Teddy had had pink, rosy cheeks; he had always been small and thin and pale, even when he was a tiny baby in Mama's arms. Then again, he was born just a few weeks after Papa died. Teddy had never known anything but lack.

Gwen couldn't bear the thought that he might die without ever knowing more.

She pushed away the very idea of death, forcing her thoughts away from it as though she could somehow fend it off by doing so. Dipping a rag back into the bucket at her side, she sponged lukewarm water over Teddy's forehead. His curls were dripping, and he made no response as she touched him. She may just as well have been invisible.

Roberta huddled, silent and pale, on one corner of the sleeping pallet. Mama lay curled on the other, sleeping an exhausted sleep. She had been nursing Teddy around the clock for four days, ever since Gwen and Roberta had first brought him back from the alleyway, soaked to the skin. The fever had started the next morning.

And it was only getting worse.

Teddy let out a quiet moan. Gwen rested a hand on his thin, bony shoulder. "Oh, Teddy," she whispered. "I wish there was something I could do."

He turned his suffering eyes to her for a moment. "Gwen," he croaked.

Gwen's heart leaped. Maybe, despite all appearances, he was getting better. This was the first time he'd spoken all day. "Teddy, darling," she said, smiling. "Are you hungry?"

Teddy stared up at her. "My chest…" He took a long, shaky breath. "It hurts."

"Just try to breathe slowly, my love," said Gwen.

Teddy took a deep breath, then began to cough, curling up on his side, saliva dripping from his dry, chapped lips. Gwen rubbed his back, terror gripping her. The cough sounded so wet and congested, and it seemed to be stealing the last of his strength.

"Teddy?" she whispered, when it stopped.

He rolled onto his back again, his eyes finding hers.

"I'm sorry," Gwen whispered, tears building behind her eyes.

Teddy stared at her for a moment longer before his eyes fluttered closed. His breathing continued, fast and laboured, and Gwen noticed that there was a bluish outline to his fingernails. She tucked his hands under the ragged blanket, trying to fight the awful desperation rising in her. What was she going to do?

"Gwen?" said Roberta.

Gwen looked over at her, forcing a smile. "Yes, Bobbie?"

Roberta's eyes filled with tears. "He's going to die, isn't he?"

Gwen stared helplessly down at the motionless figure of her little brother, listening to his rapid breathing. And she remembered Joey. She remembered him crouching down to crawl under the machine at the cotton mill, flashing a smile at her over his shoulder as he went, all of eight years old and the light of her life. She remembered the twang of a breaking thread, turning away to piece it back together. And then the terrible scream. And the thuds.

And the silence.

And the blood.

Gwen's heart was hammering at the memory. She shook her head, hard, as if she could dislodge it somehow, and pushed herself to her feet. "No," she said. "He's not. I'm going to make sure of it."

"What are you doing?" said Roberta. "Where are you going?"

"I'm going to get medicine for Teddy," said Gwen.

"How? We have no money," said Roberta.

Gwen opened the wooden box that contained all of their possessions, retrieving the few coins that lay in the bottom corner.

"That's for the rent!" gasped Roberta.

"I don't care." Gwen clutched the coins firmly. "I'm going to save him."

Before Roberta could protest, she shoved aside the curtain and marched out of the tenement, her jaw grimly set.

~ ~ ~ ~ ~

The same rain that had made Teddy sick was still falling as Gwen hurried towards the nearest apothecary. It was bitterly cold, and Gwen could feel it trickling down the back of her neck, sliding against her flesh. But she couldn't care about that now. All she cared about was saving Teddy.

The apothecary's shop was a small, miserable building hunkered down in a corner between the slums. Gwen had no idea how the shop made any money at all; if the rest of the people who lived in these slums suffered the way she did, then they had no money for medicine, either. But perhaps they, too, were driven to desperation the way she was now.

She paused in front of the door, peering through the grimy windows. The apothecary's name had once been on the door in brass letters, but it had rubbed out by now. The door was closed, but she could see light inside the building. The apothecary was in – he opened his shop for a couple of hours every Sunday, knowing that the factory workers who lived in the slums had no other time to go to the shops.

Squaring her shoulders, Gwen clutched the coins a little tighter and pushed open the door.

The shop was small and dingy, with shelves of bottles and packets crowding closely around her as she walked up to the counter at the back of the building. Behind it, the apothecary himself was as crowded and dingy as his shop; he wore little round spectacles whose lenses were smudged with grime, and between his bushy beard and the overgrown mop of his grey hair, his large, hooked nose looked like it was being squashed under the spectacles.

He watched her with simmering disgust as she approached. She stopped a few feet from the counter, clearing her throat nervously. "Hello, sir?" she attempted.

"What do you want?" snapped the apothecary. "Spit it out, child. As if it isn't bad enough that I have to work on a Sunday, now you have to drag out the process as much as you can, too!"

"No, sir, I – I just want some medicine, please, sir," stammered Gwen.

"Of course you want medicine. This is an apothecary, isn't it?" snapped the man. "Now tell me what you want."

"My little brother is sick. He's feverish and coughing," said Gwen. "Please, I just – "

"Do you have money?" the apothecary demanded.

"Oh, yes, sir!" Gwen quickly stepped up to the counter and put the money down on its surface.

The apothecary glared at it, and then at her. "And what do you expect to buy with that pittance?" he asked.

Gwen's heart failed within her. "Sir, it's all I have," she said.

"Of course it is." He waved a hand at her. "Go away. I can't help you."

"Sir, please – "

"I told you to go!" The apothecary reached under the counter, his eyes flashing. "Or must I set my dogs on you?"

Blinded by tears, Gwen scooped up the money, tucked it into her pocket, and turned to go. As she stumbled towards the door, a bottle caught her eye. It was a thing of beauty, made from deep purple glass, rounded and curvy. There was a picture on the label of a child drinking it, and a wave of absolute desperation rushed over Gwen.

She moved almost before she could think. Her hand reached out, and she snatched the bottle and bolted.

"Hey! HEY!" roared the apothecary. "STOP!"

Tears choked Gwen's throat, but she kept running, fleeing from the apothecary and from the overwhelming conviction that she was doing something terrible.

"Get back here!" The door banged behind her as she fled into the street; the apothecary was at her heels. "Stop! Stop thief!"

The street were busy, and people turned to stare as Gwen bolted past them, running with all of her faltering strength, the bottle clutched tightly to her chest. The apothecary's thumping footsteps were growing closer and closer. Gwen redoubled her pace, swung down a side street and kept running.

"STOP!" bellowed the apothecary.

Suddenly, Gwen's dress sprang tight around her ribs, a firm hand snatching at the cloth. She yelped, struggled; a second hand clawed at her arm.

"Got you!" growled the apothecary.

"No!" Gwen cried, wrenching herself free. Something ripped in her dress, and she spun out of his grip, but he still had a hold on her arm and her hand was wrenched back and her wet fingers slid across the glass surface of the bottle.

Gwen's heart froze. For a moment, as the bottle fell, it sparkled from the tiny diamond drops of rain on the purple glass to the shattering of light on the churning liquid inside. Then it met the paving, and it shattered. Shards of glass spun in every direction, and the precious liquid spilled out onto the ground.

The apothecary's hand on her arm tightened like an iron claw. "You'll pay for that!" he roared.

Tears were coursing down Gwen's cheek, but the sound of his voice seemed to speak straight to her animal instincts, instincts that told her to break free and run. She twisted again, ignoring a wrenching pain in her shoulder, and his hand slipped off her wet arm. Then she bolted, sobbing, blinded by tears, running towards home with nothing to give her little brother.

Chapter Three

Gwen was shivering uncontrollably. Her wet clothes were dripping a pool around her where she sat on the bare, rough boards of the tenement floor; it was more than an hour since she had come home from her unsuccessful bid to find medicine for Teddy, but the meagre fire in their tiny stove was doing nothing to warm or dry her. There was a dangerous tickle in the back of her throat, and her nose wouldn't stop running.

But none of that worried her now. Her entire being was focused on Teddy.

The little boy's labouring body seemed to be fighting now for every breath. He lay on the sleeping pallet, glassy-eyed, staring up at nothing as he struggled to breathe; every gasp rattled terribly through his lungs as though there was an army of disease waiting inside every tube and airway to fight against the passage of life-giving oxygen.

The ravaging fever had given way to a cold that terrified Gwen. She reached out with a trembling hand to touch his bare foot where it stuck out from under the blankets. Just hours ago, it had been burning to the touch. Now it felt terribly cold, and it was very blue.

Sweat trickled down Teddy's emaciated face, running deep into the hollows of his eye sockets and his cheekbones. His hands were limp on the sacking blanket on either side of him, but occasionally his fingers strained into fists as though he could drag the air inside himself with them.

Mama was stretched out beside Teddy. There was no more frantic sponging of his burning brow now; she seemed to know that he was far beyond help. Now, she just stroked his hair over and over again, soaked with sweat though it was, and murmured a combination of desperate prayers and insubstantial assurances that everything would be all right.

But it wouldn't be. Gwen knew it wouldn't, as surely as she had known that Joey was dead when they retrieved him from under the deadly machine. She wanted to flee. She wanted to fly to her feet, run down the stairs and rush into the city; she would face whatever fate awaited her rather than watch another brother die. But she couldn't leave her family.

Even if it meant having her heart torn open once more.

The night wore on. The cold seeped down into Gwen's bones; she stopped dripping, but her clothing still felt unbearably damp and cold against her skin. Teddy's breathing grew more and more stertorous, each terrible gasp sucking through his body. The breaths came quicker and quicker until he was pop-eyed with effort, his shoulders, hips, neck, and back all toiling with every breath, muscles jumping unnaturally in his little body.

Roberta was huddled in a corner, weeping and weeping. Mama's desperate whispers of love became more and more frightened, and she wrapped her arms around Teddy's body, pleading with him, tears coursing down her cheeks.

As his breaths came faster, Gwen turned to Roberta and wrapped her arms around her sister. "Don't watch," she whispered, pressing Roberta's face against her check. "Just don't watch."

Roberta clung to Gwen and cried, but Gwen could not tear her eyes away. The breaths began to come slower and slower; it was terrifying and relieving at the same time. Teddy's eyelids began to flutter, and the terrified look left him. He started to take tiny sips of air, ragged and exhausted.

Finally, somewhere well after midnight, Teddy turned his eyes on his mother. He reached up towards her with a small, thin hand.

"Teddy?" Mama whispered.

Teddy's fingertips brushed against Mama's cheeks. His lips twitched, as though he was trying to smile, and then his eyes fell closed and his bony hand fell to his chest. He took one more breath, and then no more.

Mama's wail split the whole night in two ragged pieces. She snatched Teddy's limp and unresisting little body into her arms and began to weep, great sobs that sounded as though they were tearing pieces out of her, wracking her entire body with grief.

Roberta's eyes were dry; she seemed relieved that it was over. Gwen got up with an effort, her joins aching with cold, and walked over to her mother. "Mama..." She reached out a hand towards her.

"Get away!" Mama's scream was harsh and loud, and it made Gwen leap back. She looked up, her eyes haggard, her hair straggling around her face. Her eyes were red and burned with fury. "Get away from me! You did this to him, do you hear me? You sent him out into the cold! You killed him!"

Each word drove home like a knife, like a slicing blade being driven into her over and over and over again until Gwen's heart felt like it was bleeding from a hundred ugly wounds. She stumbled backwards as though she'd been struck, appalled, not because her mother's words were so harsh, but because they were so unbearably true.

"Gwen..." Roberta began.

Gwen turned away, her pain overwhelming her. "I'll see you at work," she choked out to Roberta, and fled.

~ ~ ~ ~ ~

Gwen didn't know if she wanted to go back home.

Her feet were carrying her that way more out of habit than anything else. They ached after her shift at the mill, but for once, the working day felt as though it had passed in the blink of an eye. Gwen could hardly believe she had ever walked out of the tenement at all; she felt as though she was still there, still watching Teddy take his last breaths.

Everything felt surreal. Gwen felt as though she was the one who had died, not Teddy, and that she was floating through the world, detached and transparent, a lost phantasm in the world of the living. People brushed against her as she stumbled down the street, but she barely felt them. She didn't even feel the sting of Worley's cane on her palm. She had made many mistakes today. She knew she was on the very brink of dismissal.

And still, Gwen couldn't find it in her heart to care. She couldn't find it in her to feel anything, except for a steady throb of agony, and a growing reluctance to return to the tenement.

It was when they turned down the street and she saw their building waiting for them, grey and shadowed in the overcast night, that she finally realized just how much she dreaded going home. Her feet stopped, and she froze in the middle of the street, staring at the building as though it was about to pounce on her.

Roberta looked up at her, tugging at her hand. "Come on, Gwen," she said. "Let's go home. It's cold out here."

Tears prickled at Gwen's eyelids. "You go on, Bobbie," she said. "I'll be right there."

Roberta wasn't fooled. She stared up at Gwen, her eyes round and afraid. "Please." She tugged again at Gwen's hand. "Let's go inside."

Gwen hung her head, overwhelmed with terror and shame. "I can't," she whispered. "I can't go in there. Not after..." She stopped.

"Mama didn't mean it," said Roberta. "Of course you didn't kill Teddy, Gwen." Tears were running down her cheeks. "It just happened. Just like Papa and Joey. It just happened."

"No, it didn't." A sob tore at Gwen's throat. "If I had never told Mama to send Teddy out begging, he would still be alive now."

"You don't know that," said Roberta. "If you hadn't sent Teddy out, then we wouldn't have been able to stay in the tenement. Perhaps more than one of us would be dead." She pulled again.

"I can't face her," said Gwen.

"I don't care!" Roberta snapped, pain and anger clashing in her voice and eyes. "Don't you understand, Gwen? We can't do this without you. We need you!"

Gwen stared down at her little sister.

"Don't you see?" Roberta cried. "It doesn't matter what you think and believe. I can't lose you today, too!" Her words were swallowed by sobs.

Gwen stared at her tear-streaked cheeks and her desperate eyes, and felt a deep guilt in the pit of her belly. She had been so wrapped in her own shame over Teddy's death all day that she hadn't seen Roberta's pain.

"Oh, Bobbie, come here." She gathered Roberta into her arms, hugging her tightly. "You won't lose me. I promise. You'll never, never lose me."

Roberta clung to her, crying her eyes out. Gwen cuddled her close. "Come on," she whispered. "Let's go home."

~ ~ ~ ~ ~

Gwen steeled herself as she pushed aside the curtain and stepped into the tenement. She was expecting Teddy's emaciated and lifeless body to still be lying there on the sleeping pallet, but when she stepped inside, she was surprised to see that Mama was sitting by the window and the sleeping pallet was empty, its threadbare blanket pulled neatly over its surface. Mama was staring out of the window, sitting very still. She was not sobbing, but a steady trail of tears was running down her cheeks.

"Mama?" said Gwen.

Mama looked over at her, and her face crumpled. Hobbling on her failing knees, she rushed over to Gwen, throwing her arms around her. "Oh, Gwendoline," she cried. "I'm so glad you're home. I was so afraid." She was shaking as she stroked Gwen's hair, clung to her body. "Oh, my darling, I'm so glad you came home."

"I'm right here, Mama," said Gwen. She felt as though her mother's love was pounding against a wall of glass, thrown up between the two of them; she knew it was there, she saw it, but she felt nothing. She gently grasped Mama's arms and pushed her away. "Are you hungry?"

Mama wiped at her tears, looking at Gwen. "Darling, please, I need you to know how sorry I am for what I said last night," she said, taking Gwen's hands. "I didn't mean it. I was... I was so hurt." A fresh rush of tears ran down her cheeks. "But I know you did everything you could for your brother, for all of us. As you always do."

Again, Gwen felt the words hitting the glass wall. They couldn't penetrate to her aching heart, but she forced a smile. "Thank you, Mama," she said. "Do you have some food?"

Mama hung her head. "I'm sorry," she whispered. "I... I needed to pay for them to take... to take him away and bury him." Her voice broke.

Gwen's heart froze. She tried not to think of strangers' hands lifting her brother's tiny body, of the hands she had held and the cheeks she had kissed lying buried under the cold earth. Instead, her thoughts fled in a more practical direction.

"Mama." She tried her best to keep her voice calm. "Did you pay the rent?"

Mama looked up at her, and the tears rushing from her eyes were the only answer Gwen needed.

"I'm sorry," she croaked.

"Don't. Please." Gwen touched Mama's arm. "Let's just sleep."

She tried her best to sound reassuring, but she could hear the marching feet of their doom like an approaching army, drawing ever closer.

~ ~ ~ ~ ~

Gwen knew that she was risking dismissal by being late to work today, but she didn't feel she had another choice.

It was Monday, a week after Teddy's death. She had sent Roberta to the cotton mill alone, hoping to spare her the beating that she knew was waiting for her once she arrived there, terrified that Worley might strike her simply because Gwen wasn't there. Even being separated from her sister for a few hours was frightening, but she knew she had to do this.

She had to face the landlord. And Mama would not. Mama had been sitting by the window, staring into space, for an entire week; the fabric she was meant to turn into clothing for the slop-shop still lay untouched on the floor by the sleeping pallet. She had retreated deep within herself, as though she was hiding from the unrelenting grief of her miserable life.

Gwen wanted to retreat, too. She wanted to hide somewhere dark and safe, somewhere that no one could ever hurt her again. Instead, she was standing on the landing outside the tenement door, shivering in the dark hallway, clutching a single coin in her fist. Without Mama's pay from the slop-shop, it was all that she could spare, even though she hadn't eaten in three days.

The creaking of the stairs alerted her to the landlord's approach. She took a deep breath, trying to find some courage, but there was none left in her heart. It seemed to take an eternity for him to climb the stairs, and he finally reached the top. He was a small man with pinched, rodent-like features and a thin moustache of straight black hairs that stuck out past the down-turned corners of his pale mouth. The stub of candle spluttering on the landing cast a flickering light that made his features seem monstrous.

"Good morning, sir," Gwen managed.

He glared at her. "It would be, if I didn't have to come down here and deal with the likes of you," he said. He held out a hand.

Gwen took a deep breath. Trembling from head to toe, she lifted the coin and dropped it into the landlord's hand.

He stared down at it, then sneered at her. "What is this?" he demanded. "Are you stupid as well as poor? Do you think you can fool me into thinking this is your rent for the week?"

"No, sir, no, I don't think that at all," said Gwen.

"Then what is the meaning of this?" snapped the landlord. "Where's the rest of my money?"

Gwen took a deep breath. "Sir, I... I... I don't have it," she stammered out.

His eyes narrowed. "Then why are you still here?" he hissed.

"Because I think I can pay you back next week, sir," said Gwen.

"You think?" The landlord shook his head. "Do you truly think that that is good enough?"

"Please, sir." Gwen blinked frantically at her gathering tears. "Please, I can get the money. I'll find a way somehow. I'll..."

The landlord held up a hand, silencing her instantly.

"I've heard it all many times before," he said brusquely. "I have a waiting list of tenants. I don't have time for this. Get out."

Cold shock rippled through Gwen's body. "Now?" she croaked.

"*Yes*, now," snapped the landlord. "Fetch your family and get out of my building. You're trespassing on my property."

"Sir!" Gwen gasped.

The landlord took a step closer to her, his hands clenching into fists. "If you raise your voice to me again, you impudent child, I will knock some manners into you," he growled. "Now get out of my building."

Gwen was shaking as she stumbled back into the tenement. Mama was sitting by the window, staring at nothing. She didn't react when Gwen started grabbing everything they owned; it wasn't much. There was a single change of clothes and the blanket. Everything else had come with the tenement.

"Mama." Gwen grabbed Mama's arm. "Mama, we have to go."

Mama looked up at her, her eyes wide and blank. "Go?" she said. "Where?"

The question loomed in Gwen's mind, huge and empty and unanswerable.

She pulled Mama to her feet. "I don't know," she said.

Chapter Four

Gwen had hidden Mama in an alley near the cotton mill for the day. She could see her huddled there in the dark, wrapped in the blanket and clutching the canvas bag of their spare clothing, barely visible in the shadows of the alley as Gwen and Roberta stepped out of the cotton mill along with the crush of other workers. Despite her shorter shift, Gwen was so tired she could barely walk. It had been so long since she had last eaten that she had stopped feeling hungry, and now simply felt weak.

Somehow, as always, Roberta still had the strength to talk, and her chatter started as they left the mill behind and moved out into the street. "I'm so glad Worley didn't dismiss you!" she gasped. "I really thought he was going to chase you off. How's your hand?"

Gwen closed it with an effort. Worley's cane had left several ugly weals on it, and she couldn't quite bunch it into a fist thanks to the swelling. "It's fine," she said.

Mama had seen them coming out. She stood up, clutching the blanket around her, and Gwen knew that she couldn't hide the truth from Roberta any longer. She stopped, stepping in front of Roberta and turning to face her, blocking her view of their mother.

"Bobbie," she said, "there's something that I have to tell you."

Roberta's eyes widened. "What is it?" she asked, fear filling her face.

Gwen swallowed hard, not knowing how to break the news. She looked over her shoulder at Mama, but their mother made no move to come closer. She just stood there, staring, her eyes as blank as if she was looking into another world.

Gwen looked back at her sister. "We couldn't pay the rent," she said. "We don't have a home anymore." Tears filled her eyes, and she fought them back, feeling her face and voice trembling. "I'm so sorry, Bobbie."

Roberta's face crumpled. "Where will we go, Gwen?" she cried. "Where will we sleep?"

Gwen had been thinking about it all day, and her exhausted mind could come up with nothing. She took Roberta's hand and gripped it, tears rushing down her cheeks. "Right here," she said, trying to keep her voice from breaking. "Right here in the alley. We'll go down to the market and... and..." She fought back a sob. "We'll get some bread, and then we'll come and sleep here, and it'll be warm, and it'll be all right."

"It doesn't look warm." Roberta was sobbing. "We only have one blanket. Gwen, how will we stay alive this winter?"

"Let's just stay alive tonight first," said Gwen.

That alone sounded all but impossible.

~ ~ ~ ~ ~

Gwen had expected that she would be incapable of sleep. Ever since Teddy's death, she had woken up several times each night, covered in sweat, even in the comparative safety of the tenement, hearing her little brother's final gasps echoing through her mind.

But somehow, even though the city was moving all around them and a cold breeze blew down the length of the alley, Gwen fell asleep the moment she had lain down on the hard ground and wrapped her arms around Roberta. They had been able to spend all of the day's wages on bread, and even though Gwen's had been halved thanks to her lateness, they were finally able to eat almost a full meal for the first time in days. Her entire body felt like it was crying with relief.

She was sleeping deeply when the sound woke her. Her eyes heavy with sleep, she sat up, feeling groggy and disoriented. Why was the wind blowing so coldly? Had one of the boards come loose from the window again?

Then the sound came again. It was a masculine voice, and it was much too close. "Here! Over here, fellas!" it shouted. "I told you we'd find something!"

Gwen was instantly as wide awake as if she had been drenched with a bucket of ice water. She grabbed at Roberta, shaking her as her eyes adjusted to the darkness. The street lamp was just too far away for her to make out more than a silhouette, but she could see that the shape at the mouth of the alley was male, and she could smell the familiar scent of alcohol rolling off his breath. She knew it well; he smelled like Mr. Brown.

Feet approached. Roberta mumbled, "Huh? What is it?"

"Wake up!" Gwen hissed. "Mama, wake up!"

A man approached, swinging a lantern, and joined his companion at the mouth of the alley. The lantern blinded Gwen, and she held up a hand against it. Mama sat bolt upright, the colour draining from her face.

"Wh-who's there?" Gwen stammered.

One of the men spat. "She's too young," he told his companion.

"Not *her*," said the other. "The older one."

There was a pause with an assessing feeling to it, one that made Gwen's skin crawl. "She'll do," grunted the man. "Grab her."

"No!" Gwen shot to her feet, grabbing the blanket and Roberta's hand. "Leave us alone!"

But the men were walking towards them as though she had no voice at all. Mama was struggling to her feet, her knees wobbling; Gwen seized her arm. "Go away!" she shrieked.

Roberta let out a long, piercing scream. Gwen glanced over her shoulder. The other end of the alley seemed a very long way away, but they had no choice. She pulled Mama's arm over her shoulders. "Run!" she cried despairingly.

Somehow, they ran. Roberta led the way, her little feet flying, filthy hair bouncing on her shoulders in the shaky lantern light. Mama was leaning on Gwen, half pulling her down, half falling over; Gwen clung to her, forcing her to keep on running, almost dragging her forward toward the alley. And the men were right behind them.

They would never have escaped if those men were sober. But mercifully, thankfully, they were not. As Gwen and Mama stumbled out into the street, a hansom cab driving much too fast came hurtling down the road towards them. Gwen saw no other choice. Grabbing Mama tightly, she hauled her into the road right in front of the cab. The driver shouted, the horse shied, and Gwen felt the huff of its hot breath on the back of her neck as she stumbled into the road, but somehow there was no impact. Their pursuers shrieked, and she heard the shatter of a lantern falling. Darkness surrounded them, and Gwen hauled Mama towards the nearest streetlamp, shouting to Roberta with the last of her breath.

They reached the streetlamp with no one following them. Mama was barely moving her feet at all anymore; Gwen was half carrying her. But they couldn't stop. They had to escape. She dragged them onward until she could drag no more, and then they all collapsed in the shadow of an empty warehouse's doorway.

With Roberta and Mama half on top of her, and her back pressing into the warehouse door, Gwen clung to her little family, gasping for breath. She could feel Roberta's heart hammering against her ribs where they dug into Gwen's stomach. Mama's breaths were huge and ragged with pain.

"I – can't – do – this," Mama gasped out, her words broken by her panting. "We can't – survive – on these – streets."

"But where else will we go?" Roberta was the only one with the breath left to cry. "Where else is there?"

Gwen knew. But the very thought made her heart feel ice cold, even though she knew there was no other way.

~ ~ ~ ~ ~

No part of London that Gwen had ever seen was beautiful in the grubby, faltering light just before dawn. She had seen the city in that light often in summertime when she walked to work with the sun still sheltering below the horizon, sending out only a few grey and hopeless rays to scout out another meaningless day. The light always looked dirty somehow, finding its way through clouds of industrial smoke and reeking miasma to gleam sullenly on the surfaces of ramshackle buildings and muddy streets, leaving deep shadows in every corner. That first sunlight was bare, and it shone heartlessly on the ugliest of the slum's details. The slum had never seemed more appalling than at that deadly hour just before dawn, when the world was at its coldest, and the city at its worst.

Yet even in the slum, Gwen had never seen anything as terrifying as the workhouse in that light before dawn.

The workhouse was in no way in the same state of disrepair as the tenement buildings that had been Gwen's home all her life; its brickwork was solid, its walls newly plastered, and its windows hole. Yet at the same time, it was the barest building she had ever seen. Everything about it was harsh and meagre and cold and sparse. A brick wall separated it from the outside world, punctuated in a few places by wrought-iron gates; everything was topped with spikes. Beyond the imposing wall, the square shape of the building rose into the grey sky, floor upon floor, with uniform windows and long straight lines that gave no quarter.

It looked like a prison. But Gwen was shivering with cold and hunger, and even those stern walls had to be better than nothing. She told herself this over and over in her mind as she led her little family up to its great iron gates.

"Gwendoline, you can't be serious." Mama's voice shook with pain; she was leaning heavily on Gwen and Roberta, her steps heavy and shuffling.

"We have nowhere else to go, Mama," said Gwen. "At least here we can have food and shelter."

"You don't know what you've done," Mama rasped. "You don't understand how awful it is in that place."

"Should we go back, Mama?" said Roberta, staring up into Mama's face.

There was a moment's tremulous silence. Then all of Mama slouched, as though the very hope and life had suddenly gone out of her.

"No," she whispered. "There is nowhere else. Gwen is right. Let's just... go in there." Her eyes were filled with tears as she looked over at Gwen. "I'm sorry, children," she whispered.

There was something deeply chilling about her tone, something that struck cold right into Gwen's bones. She wondered what it was that Mama knew about the workhouse that she didn't. Perhaps they should go back. Perhaps even the fate that awaited them in the city would be better than...

"Good morning! How can I help you?"

The voice was absolutely unexpected. In all her life, Gwen had known only harshness from the outside world; the only love and joy she'd ever known came from her own little family. Hearing the kind and cheerful voice on a morning like this was as shocking as a ray of brilliant sunlight on a wet day, sending a rainbow of hope leaping up in her heart.

She spun around. A boy was standing behind the gates of the workhouse, regarding her with a steady, warm smile that caused a deep dimple to appear in his left cheek. He was perhaps a little older than Gwen, maybe fourteen or fifteen, and he had an endearing tousle of honey-coloured hair, paired with eyes as deeply brown as chocolate.

"You look cold and hungry," said the boy. He lifted a gigantic keyring, inserted a long key into the lock, and swung the gates open. "Do you want to come in?"

There was genuine concern in his eyes as they ran over Gwen and Roberta with their ragged clothes and broken shoes, and over Mama, leaning on Roberta with her trembling limbs about to give way underneath her.

Suddenly, looking into the boy's gentle face, Gwen yearned to go into that workhouse.

Mama seemed to feel the same way. Her face was haggard with defeat, her voice trembling and quiet. "Yes," she croaked. "Yes, please, we need to come in."

"Please, come." The boy hurried over and held out his hands to Mama. "Let me help you, miss. You must be exhausted."

"Thank you," breathed Roberta, stepping back as the boy drew Mama's arm over his shoulder. Gwen could hardly believe it as the boy walked on ahead of them, helping Mama limp up to the tall and imposing door of the workhouse. Were they really coming in out of the cold? Was it possible that things would truly get better for them now?

The boy paused at the door, looking over his shoulder, and now there was a hint of sorrow in his eyes. "I'm sorry it's come to this for you," he said softly. "But it will all get better. At least now you're all safe."

"What do you mean, 'at least'?" said Gwen.

Before the boy could answer, the door swung open, and a woman was standing there who was as square and cold as the workhouse itself. Her eyes were so pale that they hardly seemed any colour at all; perhaps they had been blue once, but the half-moon spectacles and her snow-white hair made them looked like their colour had been washed clean away.

"What's this, Nicholas?" she barked.

"New intakes, ma'am," said the boy. "Please, they're cold and hungry, be kind to them."

"Kind!" The woman shook her head. "There's no kindness to spare here." She glared down at Gwen, who felt suddenly very small and insignificant. "You'd better come in," she snapped. "This way. My name is Mrs. Webb. I'm the matron of this workhouse."

Gwen was too afraid to disobey. Mrs. Webb led them down a dark, narrow hallway to a cold room lit by a square of sunlight and a feeble gas lamp. There was a table on one side of the room with a few sets of folded clothing on it; on the other was a bathtub, with copper pipes and taps. Gwen had never seen taps for a bathtub before, only in the cotton mill itself. She stared at them.

Mrs. Webb went over and opened both taps. Water gushed into the tub, and some of it was steaming. The sight of the hot water made Gwen feel even colder. She had never bathed in hot water before.

"You two girls. Take off your clothes," said Mrs. Webb.

The boy had excused himself; it was just Mrs. Webb and Gwen and Roberta and Mama. Gwen thought she had heard wrong. "I beg your pardon?" she said.

"Take off your clothes. Quickly," snapped Mrs. Webb. "We don't need your lice in here."

Mama hesitated, but Roberta was eyeing the hot water, and she pulled her ragged dress over her head without a second thought. Goosebumps rose on her flesh; Gwen hated how she could see every bone in Roberta's spine as she stepped towards the bath, naked and shivering, her arms wrapped around herself. Mrs. Webb closed the taps, and Roberta slid into the bath, letting out a gasp and staring at Gwen with wide eyes.

"It's warm!" she gasped.

"Come on," said Mrs. Webb. "We don't have all day."

Gwen found herself peeling off her own clothes, eager to get into that warm water. It had already turned muddy brown from Roberta's filth when she got in, but there was still something inexpressibly soothing about the way it lapped around her body. She plunged her head underneath it, working the hot water through her long black hair; Mrs. Webb gave them a cake of hard soap, and she fought with it to form a lather on her hair. Dirt came off in chunks; she worked her fingers through the strands, trying to separate them.

When Gwen sat up, feeling clean despite the brown colour of the bathwater she was sharing with Roberta, Mama was staring down at the floor, her cheeks very red. Now that Gwen was a little warmer, she felt suddenly grotesque, sitting here naked in front of this stranger.

Mrs. Webb had turned away, and she came back with two ugly dresses draped over her arm. They were both very bare and had been mended many times, and they were black and white, with ugly vertical stripes. "Get dressed," she snapped.

Gwen didn't want to get out of the wonderfully hot water, but Mrs. Webb made it evident that there was no denying her. She quickly stepped out and stood shivering while Mrs. Webb handed her a tiny, hard towel. It was impossible to dry herself completely with it, and she was still damp and shivering when she pulled the dress over her head. It felt sturdier than her own dress, but also harder and scratchy.

"I liked my dress better," said Roberta, looking up at Mrs. Webb with wide eyes.

"Your dress will be incinerated," snapped Mrs. Webb. "Now come with me."

She headed for the door, and Roberta started after her, but Gwen stopped in the middle of the floor.

"Wait," she said. "What about Mama?"

Mrs. Webb didn't even look at her as she held the door for Roberta to walk through.

"Your mother will go with the women," she says. "You two are going to be with the girls."

Horror rose up in a dark, sucking tide, engulfing Gwen, filling her mouth and nose and dragging her under.

"You're going to separate us?" she cried.

"What? No!" Roberta spun around. "Don't take me away from my mama!"

But Mrs. Webb was too quick. Her fist closed on Roberta's thin arm, yanking her back. "Stop your noise, child!" she barked. "This is how it is in the workhouse."

"No. No!" shrieked Roberta. "NO!"

Gwen felt dizzy with horror and shock. She had brought them here to keep them safe and together, not to have them torn apart from one another.

"Silence!" roared Mrs. Webb, shaking Roberta hard. "Come now!" She turned, physically dragging Roberta with her.

"No! No! Mama! Gwen!" Roberta screamed.

Helpless and panicking, Gwen turned to look at Mama. But Mama's eyes were hollow and empty, as though hardship had scooped the very heart out of her body.

"Go with your sister, Gwendoline," she whispered.

"Mama…" Gwen croaked, tears stinging as they ran down her cheeks.

"Just go." Mama dropped her eyes to the floor.

Gwen had no choice. She turned away from her mother and followed her sister's screams into the dark belly of the workhouse.

Part Two

Chapter Five

Two Years Later

Gwen kept a close eye on Roberta as the two of them hurried across the crowded dining hall. It was filled with a steady hubbub of chatter as hundreds of girls sat down for breakfast, or rather, for the cold and unsatisfactory excuse for breakfast that the workhouse always gave them.

Two years ago, before Gwen and Roberta had come to the workhouse, Gwen might have given anything for three meals a day – meagre though they were. Yet now, there were times when she wished that she had never brought her family to this terrible place.

She kept her eyes on Roberta's bowl, an arm wrapped around her younger sister's shoulders, as they hastened to the table at the far end of the room. They had to pass by several other tables to do so; all of them were crowded, and she could feel the hungry eyes of all the other girls following them as they walked. As always, Gwen tried her best to keep her head down. Avoiding eye contact could mean avoiding trouble. Instead, she watched the blob of cold gruel at the bottom of Roberta's bowl. It was putty grey, and wobbled as they walked; perhaps it would have turned a less hungry stomach, but Gwen found herself fixating on it as they walked towards their table.

With the eyes of every other girl upon them, the distance felt interminable. Gwen held Roberta close, forcing herself not to look up, even though she wished she could see trouble coming. There was never a question of whether or not there would be trouble. The question was which quarter the trouble would come from...

As usual, it happened just as they passed the last table before their own, the one second from the end. A foot reached out as they squeezed past in the narrow gap between the table and the wall, and Roberta stumbled. Gwen moved like a snake. She snatched the bowl out of her sister's hands, keeping the precious food from landing on the ground, and Roberta fell headlong on her hands and knees.

"Oh!" Roberta yelped in pain.

Gwen felt a twist of guilt in her heart, but she knew that a little tumble was much better than going hungry all morning. She dragged her eyes up from the floor and met the cold blue gaze of June Harrington, one of the oldest girls. Looking at June, it was almost difficult to believe that she was a workhouse waif at all. There was a wispy, otherworldly beauty to her teardrop-shaped face and white-blonde hair, even though it hung around her face in swampy fronds. She had the beauty of some wild thing, some marsh phantom that rose from the mists to lure unwary travellers to their deaths.

Her eyes betrayed it all. They were a blue so dark they were nearly black, and held nothing but danger.

She tipped back her chin. "Trying to sneak past without paying the toll, are you?"

Gwen knew it was fruitless, but she tried in any case. "Please, June," she said, her voice quavering. "Bobbie's hungry."

"Well, if she's hungry, then it doesn't matter if you lose one plate, does it?" June's eyes flashed to the two wooden bowls in Gwen's hands.

Gwen glanced helplessly towards the table at the far end of the room, where Mrs. Webb and maid were serving the last few girls' breakfast. She knew from experience that unless actual blood was drawn, Mrs. Webb was highly unlikely to get involved in their conflict. Briefly, she considered trying to push past, or to shove June aside. The girl looked thin and wispy enough to knock over with a feather. But she knew, also from experience, that she could bite and scratch like a wildcat if she felt like it.

Shaking in her cheap shoes, Gwen held out one of the bowls.

"Thank you," said June, with syrupy sweetness. "That wasn't so hard, now, was it?" She took the bowl and sat back down at the table, where all the other girls drew back from her, and began to eat in ravenous gulps.

Gwen's stomach cramped with longing at the sight, but she forced herself to turn away, bending down to grab Roberta's arm. "Come on," she hissed, pulling her sister to her feet. "Let's go."

Roberta clung to her, snivelling, as Gwen led her to the empty table. They huddled side by side and Gwen pushed the remaining bowl of gruel over to Roberta. "There, there, Bobbie," she said, rubbing her sister's back through the coarse workhouse dress that was already much too small. "There's a good girl. Eat your breakfast now."

"But you'll be h-h-h-hungry," choked Roberta, her breath catching on sobs.

"I'm just fine. Go on." Gwen knew that if her sister didn't start eating now, she wouldn't be able to resist the temptation to take a few bites. "Have your breakfast before it gets too cold."

Roberta lifted the cheap tin spoon and started gulping down the gruel, one giant mouthful at a time. In a matter of seconds, it was all gone. She laid the spoon aside and licked the bowl clean, meticulously catching every last scrap of food.

"There. Isn't that better?" Gwen mustered up a smile.

Roberta looked up at her with red, running eyes and nodded.

"Ah, Bobbie, why are you crying?" Gwen ran the back of her hand over the little girl's cheek. "We're going to have a nice day. We're going to go to lessons now, and then it'll be lunch." *Lunch* – it would be her first meal in twenty-four hours, thanks to June. And after that would be chores. Gwen's heart fluttered at the thought of chores; they were the only light in her life.

"It's not going to be a nice day. We haven't had a single nice day in this workhouse since we came here, Gwen," said Roberta miserably. "Lessons are awful. June keeps trying to get me into trouble. I haven't learned a thing. I don't know how you picked up your bit of reading."

"Oh, Bobbie, don't worry," said Gwen, her heart breaking. "I'll keep you safe from June."

"I know you try." Roberta sighed and lowered her arms onto the table, pillowing her head on them. "I miss Mama," she mumbled into the crook of her arm.

Tears stung Gwen's eyes.

"Me too, Bobbie," she whispered. "Me too."

~ ~ ~ ~ ~

Mopping out the workhouse hallway was a task that most girls avoided like the plague, especially now, with autumn reaching frosty fingers across the city. The entire workhouse was bleak and cold as a rule, but nowhere was worse than that hallway by the front door. An icy wind always blew under the door and none of the girls' skirts were long enough to full cover their ankles, allowing that chill air to blast through one's stockings and freeze one to the very bones.

But for Gwen, the hallway was the only place where she had ever found joy in the entire workhouse, and not because of the work. She was always the first – and only – girl to volunteer for the task. The exhausted matron didn't care why; she just pointed Gwen to the mop and bucket, and told her to go.

Now, cold water sloshed in the bucket as Gwen walked up the hallway, the mop tucked under her arm. There wasn't enough soap in the water and the mop's handle gave her splinters, but she didn't care.

She turned the corner in the hallway, and saw him at once, standing by the door and peering through the tiny window at the top. Nicholas Jones. She paused for a moment in the corner, admiring him silently; the strong lines of his shoulders, growing broad despite his thin frame; the tousle of his golden hair underneath his cap. He was wearing a woolly blue scarf, and his hands were clasped behind his back, showing his finger-less black gloves.

"Morning," said Gwen, very softly.

Nicholas spun around. His wide brown eyes softened the moment they rested on her, and he hastened over to her. "Hello, Gwen," he said.

Her name rolled off his tongue as softly as honey, and she loved the way he said it. She smiled up at him; it was always Nicholas who could make her smile, even at a time like this.

"It's always good to see you, Nicholas," she said.

"Please – I've told you. Call me Nick." He smiled. "Can I carry the bucket for you?"

"Yes, please," said Gwen.

Her hand was shaking as he took the bucket from it, and he glanced at her, concern flashing across his face. "Don't tell me that that June girl has been stealing food from you again," he said.

"I'm afraid so." Gwen sighed, following him as he placed the bucket near the door. She plunged the mop into it and started working on the floor, knowing that chatting with the porter might be a crime Mrs. Webb was willing to overlook, but idleness certainly was not.

"That girl." Nick shook his head angrily.

"I wish Mrs. Webb would do something about her," said Gwen.

"Mrs. Webb can't be bothered," said Nick, irritation in his voice. "Besides, she's grooming June to be hired out over Christmastide; she thinks she'll find work easily as a maid." His voice relented a little. "But let's not think about such things now. Tell me how your sister is."

"She's all right. Well, as much all right as she can be." Gwen smiled. "At least she's not hungry anymore, not like she was when we were working in the cotton mill. That's one good thing about being here in the workhouse."

"I know the workhouse is an awful place, but I would have died on the streets without it," said Nick.

Gwen glanced up at his friendly face as she mopped, then asked the question slowly, hesitantly. "How old were you," she asked, "when you... well... when you came here."

"Five," said Nick. "My father was never part of my life, and my mother abandoned me on a street corner. I tried to get by with begging and such, but when winter came, I was dying. The police brought me here."

Gwen stared up at him, feeling a strange sense of shame wash over her. She had always had a family; Nick couldn't even remember his own.

"It's no surprise that this place is better for you, then," she said.

"I know it's hard being away from your mother, but the streets are a terrible place to be." Nick shuddered. "Anything is better than that. And here there are a few opportunities. Like me – I worked my way up to being the porter here."

"I suppose." Gwen sighed, going back to her work. "I just want to be a family again."

"I understand that." Nick smiled, leaning against the wall, keeping an eye out through the window to see if anyone was coming past. "One day I'll have a family all my own," he said quietly.

Gwen glanced at him, surprised, but kept listening as she worked.

"I'll have a lovely wife," he said softly, "and a little home – something cosy and small and lovely, and all my own. And we'll have children, and grandchildren, and aunts and uncles..." He let out a long, fluttering sigh of pure longing.

That future seemed far too beautiful even to dream of. Out of everyone Gwen knew in this dark and awful place, Nick was the only one with the courage left to dream.

~ ~ ~ ~ ~

Somehow, Gwen and Roberta had managed to get past June and all of the other bullies the next morning. They were sitting in the comparative peace of the far table; it was crowded with the littler girls, all of them between the ages of seven and fourteen, and some of them clearly had never been taught how to eat at a table before. They sucked and slurped and drank straight from their bowls and dragged their grubby sleeves over their filthy mouths; they shouted and talked over one another and shrieked and cried, but at least they left Gwen and Roberta alone. For now, that would have to count as peace.

Roberta was gulping down her bread and jam as quickly as she could. Even though it was dry rye bread, and lumpy jam, Gwen did her best to make it last as long as possible, savouring every bite. With June around, it was impossible to tell when her next meal would come, so she took one tiny bite at a time and chewed it slowly, trying to get every drop of sweetness. Perhaps that would fool her stomach into thinking she was eating her fill, even though that was quite impossible here in the workhouse.

The soothing motion of chewing was starting to make her feel better. Even though the food wasn't much, it was enough to allay the ache of hunger in her belly a little. She managed a real smile for Roberta for the first time in days.

"I'm so glad you're having breakfast, too, Gwen," said Roberta, lighting up at the sight of Gwen's smile.

Gwen forced herself to act casual. "Yes, it's nice," she said, then steered the subject away. "So, can I help you with your letters again at lessons today? You did so well yesterday. Your As and Bs were lovely."

"Yes please, Gwen." Roberta gave a tremulous smile. "Maybe if June is too busy picking on poor little Maggie again, I can keep making a little bit of progress."

Progress. Gwen's heart stung at the word; it was what she wanted most for Roberta, yet it seemed so far out of reach. She wanted, *needed* Roberta to learn her letters. Every little piece of knowledge her sister could accumulate might just be enough to give her a better future. A future with three meals a day, and no prospect of the workhouse. Her heart ached with longing for that distant dream.

Mrs. Webb's voice resounded through the dining hall like the dread crack of a whip. Gwen and Roberta both jumped, and Gwen crammed the rest of her bread hastily into her mouth, lest it be taken from her.

"Attention!" barked Mrs. Webb.

There was silence. The girls ignored their teachers often, but no one dared to do anything but listen silently when Mrs. Webb spoke.

She was standing at the far end of the room now, glaring down into a small notebook she held in one hand. "Which one of you is Gwendoline Hopewell?" she demanded.

Gwen felt as though her bones had turned to ice. She sat very still, trembling, her mouth still full of bread. Roberta gave her a wide-eyed look, terror blazing in her pinched little face.

"Well?" snapped Mrs. Webb. "I know she's not dead. Her name is still in my ledger."

"If it pleases you, Mrs. Webb," said June sweetly, giving a simpering little smile, "I know which one she is." She pointed right at Gwen. "She's over there."

Gwen couldn't move; she was frozen with fear. What could it be? Her thoughts fled to her mother, and everything inside her quailed. If something had happened to Mama, would Mrs. Webb even care enough to tell Gwen about it? It was intolerable to live in the same building as her mother, and yet never see her; she hadn't glimpsed Mama once in the two years since she had come here.

Mrs. Webb strode over to their table, her shoes clicking ominously on the cold stone floor. She glared down at Gwen. "Well, is it true?" she said. "Are you Gwendoline Hopewell?"

Gwen swallowed her mouthful of bread. Silence would be dubbed insubordination, and the consequences for that were appalling. "Yes, ma'am," she breathed.

"Very well." Mrs. Webb turned away. "Come with me."

Gwen got up on shaking legs. She walked towards the matron, aware that Roberta was right behind her. Mrs. Webb strode off without looking back, and the two girls scurried after her. Gwen knew every girl in the dining hall was watching her, and that none of them envied whatever fate awaited her.

They reached the door, and Mrs. Webb pushed it open, turning around. "Go on, then," she said to Gwen. Then her eyes turned to Roberta. "Get back to your seat, child," she spat.

"That's my sister," Roberta quavered. "Where are you taking her?"

Mrs. Webb frowned at her. "I told you to get back to your seat."

"Please, ma'am." Gwen was shaking head to foot with fear. "Please, where are we going?"

Mrs. Webb sighed, turning to Gwen. "You're fourteen years old now. It's time you joined the women and started pulling your own weight."

Gwen felt as though a bucket of ice water had been thrown down the back of her dress. She gasped, trembling, staring up at Mrs. Webb, speechless. She knew that to join the women was to leave Roberta behind – completely alone, in a sea of girls like June.

"Now come along," snapped Mrs. Webb.

"No!" Roberta's shriek was a raw, deafening cry that echoed through the dining hall. She flung herself forward, wrapping both hands around Gwen's wrist. "No! No! No! You can't take her! You can't take my Gwen!"

"Bobbie!" Gwen gasped, grabbing her sister's hands.

"Stop that racket at once!" roared Mrs. Webb, seizing the back of Roberta's dress. "Let her go!"

"No! Bobbie! Bobbie!" Gwen snatched at Roberta's hands. "Don't let go. Don't let go!" Her entire body was thrilling with utter panic.

"Stop it. Stop your noise!" shouted Mrs. Webb. "Josephine, get over here!"

One of the maids came running; a wide-eyed girl who had grown up in the workhouse herself.

"Take the little one," barked Mrs. Webb. "And be sure not to give her any supper for this insolence."

"Gwen!" shrieked Roberta.

Tears were pouring down Gwen's cheeks as Josephine grabbed Roberta's dress and yanked her away. She knew that to fight any harder would result in a far worse punishment for Roberta than one single missed meal. Sobbing wholeheartedly, she let go of her sister's arms.

"No! Gwen! Gwen!" screamed Roberta.

"I'll find you, Bobbie!" Gwen cried. Already, Josephine was ragging Roberta bodily into the dining hall. "I'll find you!"

The dining hall door slammed, and Gwen was alone with Mrs. Webb in the hallway. Sobbing, she looked up at the matron, and saw her face twist with fury. She drew back a bony hand and struck Gwen across the face with a force that made her stagger back against the wall. Pain blinded her, and blood filled her mouth, hot and salty.

"Find her?" snapped Mrs. Webb. "Find her? You will do no such thing, child. You will do as you are told – and only as you are told – or face the consequences." She grabbed Gwen's shoulders in two cold, hard hands and glared into her face. "Is that understood?" she hissed, her breath reeking.

Gwen swallowed a mouthful of blood. She couldn't speak past the pain and the tears, but she forced herself to nod.

Chapter Six

As Mrs. Webb led her away from the dining hall, Gwen's only hope was that Mama might be among the group of women she was going to join. Roberta's screams were still echoing in her mind, and tears continued to pour down her cheeks as she followed Mrs. Webb down the long hallway. They passed the hall leading to the front door; Gwen glanced up, and saw Nick standing there. When he saw her, his eyes widened, but neither of them dared to speak.

The workhouse was larger than it had seemed from the outside. Gwen had spent the past two years living in the same few rooms: dormitory, dining hall, classroom, and a small courtyard where they could sit in the sunlight sometimes. Even when the girls were tasked with cleaning the building, it was only in the hallways near to their quarters. Now, they were leaving behind the rooms that had been Gwen's world for two full years. It seemed like Mrs. Webb was leading her further and further away from the front door, towards the back of the building, and Gwen despaired of seeing Nick again, too.

But if she could see Mama… oh, if she could only run into her mother's arms, and feel that embrace one more time, perhaps everything would be better.

They had reached a door; beyond it, Gwen could hear the thumping and churning of some kind of industry. Mrs. Webb pushed it open, motioning for her to go inside. Quivering, Gwen stepped forward into a giant room filled with steam.

It was an enormous laundry. Gwen had never seen so many clothes all in one place before. She knew that she herself had two sets of clothes, and that one of them was always off being washed, and came back to her clean; it had never occurred to her what a vast undertaking it must be to wash those hundreds of suits of clothing for all the workhouse inmates. There were great stubs of steaming water, and long lines of drying clothing everywhere. And all of them were being worked by crews of sweating women in the same striped dresses and white bonnets as those that were being washed.

Blinking away her surprise, Gwen began to search eagerly among the faces of the women that were present. Her mother had to be among them. She had to.

"Well, don't just stand there, child," spat Mrs. Webb. "Get to work." She placed the flat of her hand against Gwen's back and shoved her forward, then marched out of the room, slamming the door behind her – sealing Gwen in the room full of strangers.

She stood there, terrified, until a woman with red cheeks and watery blue eyes motioned to her. "Come over here," she said. "We could use another scrubber."

"Yes, ma'am. Of course, ma'am." Gwen hurried over to the woman. Along with several others, she was standing around a great tub filled with soapy water, scrubbing one dress after the other. Gwen reached her hands into the tub, and yelped when the water scalded her skin.

"They can't run a hot bath for the inmates here, but they always made the water much too hot for the laundry," muttered one of the women angrily.

Gwen forced a tremulous smile, plunging her hands more deeply into the soapy water. Ignoring the sting of hot water on chapped hands, she grabbed at a floating shirt and started to scrub it as well as she could.

"That's it," said the red-cheeked woman. "Keep going."

The few words of encouragement were just enough to give Gwen the courage to ask. "My... my mother should be here," she said.

The woman glanced at her, then at the others. "Oh?" she said, her voice flat and disinterested. "What was her name?"

Was. The past tense made Gwen shudder.

"B-Bertha," she said. "Bertha Hopewell. She has awful knock knees." She swallowed. "Do any of you know her?"

Without meeting her eyes, the other women shook their heads. Gwen felt that she wanted to cry. How could no one here know her mother?

"Please," she said, hearing her voice crack. It felt as though the world was stretching all around her, huge and empty and cold, without Roberta at her side. "Please, are you all sure?"

"I'm quite sure," said the red-cheeked woman, her voice relenting a little. "But I've been here ten years and I've never known a Bertha Hopewell. Perhaps she's just in the other group of women; there are two of us, you know."

"She is?" Gwen gasped. "Do they share a dormitory?"

"No." The red-cheeked woman shook her head. "But try not to talk too much, child. Get to work."

Gwen hung her head, going back to her scrubbing. She tried her best to cling to the tiny drop of hope that the woman had given her, but it was a very small piece of hope, and the world was so big and so filled with loneliness and total despair.

~ ~ ~ ~ ~

Gwen tried to lie as still as possible, even though there was a persistent itch in her left ankle, undoubtedly from the thin mattress on which she was lying. It was infested with bed bugs; small bites littered Gwen's body every morning, itching intolerably. She wanted nothing more than to scratch her ankle, but she knew that movement would wake Linda, the girl who shared the narrow bunk bed with her. Linda mostly ignored the fact that Gwen existed, but last time Gwen had kicked her in the midst of a terrifying nightmare, she had threatened to throw Gwen right out of bed and onto the cold floor for the night.

Gwen glanced down at the stone floor and shuddered. It was so cold; even here, on the bottom bunk, her breath steamed in the air.

She'd grown accustomed to sharing a bed with others, of course. It was all she'd ever known. But at least, back in the tenements, and even in the workhouse dormitory with the other girls, it had always been Roberta's dear little body that she had held close; the proximity of another had been family, had been security and warmth. But sleeping next to Linda, who had been a stranger only four days ago, was almost unbearable. At least Linda never tried to pinch or push her, but having her in the same bed still felt like an invasion.

She wondered who would be sharing Roberta's bunk now. The thought sent tears stinging to her eyes. She could only hope that it was one of the little girls, someone small and hungry and harmless who wouldn't do anything to Roberta. But what if it was June? What if it was one of the bigger girls, a girl who would force her out of bed and make her sleep on the floor? Was June stealing all of Roberta's meals, without Gwen to protect her? Would she ever make any progress in her lessons?

Tears trickled down Gwen's cheeks. The pressure of these questions seemed to be crushing her. She had to see Roberta. She had to make sure her little sister was all right, or the consequences could be dire. No one had ever actually starved to death, that Gwen knew of, in this workhouse; but she had seen girls grow thinner and weaker until consumption simply took them.

The thought of that happening to Roberta was too much. Gwen had to see her. Slowly, she pushed back the single, thin blanket and rolled out of bed as silently as she could. Linda stirred, but didn't wake. The stone floor was icy to her bare feet, but she dared not pause to put on her shoes. Holding her breath, Gwen tiptoed across the long dormitory. All around her, women were sleeping in twos and threes, crammed into the narrow beds; some of them snored, others simply breathed with difficulty. But none of them woke. Gwen made it to the door on the other side of the room.

She tried the handle, knowing it would not be locked; the disgusting lavatory was on the other side of the hallway. It opened slowly, with a long, ominous creak. Gwen froze, but there was no sound from the women. Letting out her breath slowly, she stepped into the hallway and eased the door shut behind her.

The hallway was absolutely dark. Gwen could smell the stench of the lavatory, and she knew that the laundry room was off to her left. To her right was the dining hall. The women and girls shared a dining hall; there was always ten minutes between their mealtimes, so that Gwen was always tantalizingly close to Roberta, but never actually saw her. She headed that way. From the dining hall, she could find her way to Roberta's dormitory.

She began to relax as she neared the dining hall, her bare feet soundless on the stone. Hope began to flicker in her heart, hope to finally hold her little sister in her arms again. If she found Roberta like this, maybe she could find Mama, too. Maybe a few midnight quests would be enough to piece their family back together again...

She took the turn to the dining hall, and a voice spoke behind her, so loud and sudden that it made Gwen jump and whirl around.

"What are you doing, child?"

Gwen trembled. A looming figure, lit up by candlelight, was standing in the hallway.

It was Mrs. Webb.

"Well?" she boomed, her voice harsher than ever at this time of night. She was holding a candle in one hand, and she wore a voluminous nightgown and a long white cap. "Where are you going?"

Gwen knew there was no lying to Mrs. Webb. "Oh, ma'am, please," she whispered, tears running down her cheeks. "I just want to see my sister. I just want to know that she's all right. Please, ma'am." She began to sob, trembling with terror. "She's the only family I have left."

"You lost your right to a family when you came to this place and became a burden on the rest of society," spat Mrs. Webb. She advanced on Gwen. "Have you forgotten the rules?"

"No, ma'am, I – " Gwen began.

Mrs. Webb's blow cut off her words. It was a terrible, backhanded slap that crashed across her face, sending a bloom of pain across her cheeks and nose, tears filling her eyes with blinding speed. Gwen stumbled backwards, falling to the ground. There was something wet and warm running down her upper lip. She dragged her hand across it and stared down at it in shock; it was blood. Her nose was bleeding.

Mrs. Webb didn't shout, but her voice trembled with suppressed anger.

"Get back to your dormitory," she hissed. "And if I catch you in these hallways at night again, I will have you in the refractory ward."

Those words struck utter terror into Gwen's soul. The refractory ward was a dark and windowless room, and she could be trapped in there alone for days if Mrs. Webb saw fit. "Yes, ma'am," she stuttered through blood and tears. Stumbling to her feet, she hurried back to her dormitory as fast as her failing legs would carry her.

~ ~ ~ ~ ~

Even the fear of the refractory ward wasn't enough to keep Gwen from trying to see her sister.

Just a few days later, she found herself tiptoeing out of the darkened dormitory once more, determined to be quieter this time, to not be caught this time. She had tried her best to convince herself to stay away. She had never been in the refractory ward herself, but she had heard the stories, and she had seen the blank eyes of the girls who had been in there for too long; they seemed shocked, empty, as though their time locked up all alone had broken their very view of the world.

But even that would be better than the constant worry that stole Gwen's sleep and even her appetite. She heard noises in the workhouse sometimes – voices – and wondered if they were Roberta's. If she was screaming for help, and no one ever came.

Gwen kept one hand on the wall as she walked, feeling her way along the hallway in complete darkness. She placed each foot carefully, her heart hammering so hard that she feared its beating alone would be enough to give her away. Every time she reached a corner or a doorway, she peered around it fearfully, and only proceeded when she was sure there was no one watching.

Each step brought her a little closer to her goal, and it was only the thought of seeing Roberta again that kept her moving at all.

At last, somehow, Gwen reached the door of the dining hall. It was a large room, and the door was just as large; a heavy bolt kept it in place, and she had never seen it closed before. With trembling hands, she reached for the bolt and slid it back. To her relief, somehow, it moved silently, and she grasped the door with both hands and pulled.

But the door didn't budge. Tears of desperation rose to Gwen's eyes. She gritted her teeth and pulled again; again, the door seemed stuck. She had to walk through the dining hall to reach the hallway leading to Roberta's dormitory. She had no choice but to try again. Bracing a bare foot on the wall, Gwen leaned back and hauled on the door with all her might.

Suddenly, it came unstuck. The door flew towards her, and Gwen fell over backwards with the force of her pull, landing heavily on her back. For a moment, she felt gratitude that the door did not creak.

Then it swung wide open and slammed deafeningly against the wall.

The sound echoed through the workhouse, resounding from room to room. Gwen scrambled to her feet, panic gripping her. She had no idea where Mrs. Webb's quarters were, but they had to be somewhere close by. Perhaps she should make a run for it back to her dormitory. But Mrs. Webb had caught her between her dormitory and the dining hall last time – her quarters had to be in that direction.

Somewhere behind her, a door banged open. "Nicholas!" yelled Mrs. Webb.

Gwen panicked. She ran forward into the dining hall; candlelight was flaring in the mouth of the hallway. She had to hide. Rushing up to the nearest of the hard wooden benches, Gwen threw herself underneath it, pressing the length of her body against the cold floor.

"Nicholas!" Mrs. Webb shouted again. The candlelight was coming closer, flickering its way into the dining hall. Gwen pressed herself against the floor as though she could melt into it somehow.

Mrs. Webb strode into the dining hall, holding the candle aloft. She squinted through her half-moon spectacles, looking short-sighted as she peered into the hall.

"Ma'am?" called a welcome voice.

Gwen had to put a hand over her mouth to keep from gasping with delight. It was Nick. He walked into the hall beside Mrs. Webb, looking rumpled and tired; it seemed as though he slept in his clothes. Gwen wondered what hours he worked.

"Someone's snooping around in the hallways, Nicholas," said Mrs. Webb. "Help me to find them. I'll search the dining hall and the children's dormitories – you go back towards the women's." She leaned forward a little, holding the candle aloft. "Although I could swear there's someone in the dining hall."

Nick peered into the shadows, and Gwen flinched back, but not quickly enough. She saw the ripple of shock run through his body when he saw her, and she held her breath, panic gripping her once more. Everything was about to go so wrong.

"No… no, Mrs. Webb, I don't see anyone," said Nick calmly.

Gwen let out the breath, daring to hope.

"Why don't you go back towards the women's dormitories, Mrs. Webb?" Nick asked. "It's a shorter walk for you. I'll search for the children."

Mrs. Webb looked up at him, and to Gwen's shock, she laid a hand on Nick's shoulder in a little motion of surprising tenderness.

"You know, Nicholas," she said, "you give me hope that some of these children can be saved." She sighed. "Go on – search the dining hall first, though."

"Yes, ma'am," said Nick.

Mrs. Webb hurried off, and as soon as the candlelight had vanished into the hallway, Nick crouched down to the ground.

"You can come out now, Gwen," he whispered.

Tear-streaked and dusty, Gwen crawled out from under the bench. Nick held out a hand to her, and she wrapped her fingers around his, raising her face to his eyes. They were so soft, and the grip on her hand was the gentlest touch she had ever known. It made something flutter deep in the pit of her stomach, something that she had never felt before.

"Nick," she breathed. It felt as though every thought in her mind had suddenly fled now that she felt his hand on her own.

"Are you all right?" Nick asked, releasing her hand.

She let it hover in the air for a moment, then clutched her skirt, her reality crashing back down over her shoulders. "Y-yes," she stammered. "I – I – I just have to see Bobbie." Tears boiled over, and she covered her face with her hands. "Oh, Nick, I just have to see Bobbie!"

"We'll have to be quick, then," Nick said.

She stopped, staring at him. "Q-quick?" she stammered.

"Yes. It'll take Mrs. Webb about ten minutes to search the hallways," said Nick. "You can see Roberta quickly, and I'll hide you under the bench again before I tell Mrs. Webb that there's no one out here.

When she's gone back to bed, you can go back to your dormitory."

Gwen stared up at him, a thousand emotions rising and clashing in her heart. "Do you mean it?" she breathed.

"Of course." Nick smiled, holding out his hand again. "Come on. Let's go. Quick!"

They hurried off through the dark hallways, and Nick was carrying no candle, yet somehow even in the pitch darkness, the touch of his hand was as brilliant a guiding light as the rays of the summer sun.

~ ~ ~ ~ ~

Gwen waited, trembling, in the hallway outside the dormitory that had been her home for two years until she was so cruelly jerked away from her sister's arms. Nick had an ear to the door, listening for anyone who might be awake; he glanced over at Gwen, giving her a quick smile, barely visible in the tiny sliver of moonlight from a chink in the curtains of the small window opposite.

"You'll have to be quick," he reminded her in a whisper. "And don't wake anyone."

"Nick…" Gwen took a deep breath. "Thank you."

"Of course. Hurry," Nick hissed, and pulled the door soundlessly open.

Gwen tiptoed inside, her heart in her mouth. She could only hope that Roberta was still sleeping in the same bunk as always; right in the back corner, where the smaller girls slept. Moving among the sleeping bodies, Gwen crouched down by their old bunk.

She knew her sister at once, even without seeing or touching her. She knew the sound of her rhythmic breathing, the smell of her curly hair.

"Roberta?" she whispered.

Something stirred. Gwen braced herself, frozen, for discovery. Then a delighted voice whispered in the dark, a voice that spoke to every corner of Gwen's heart.

"Gwen?" Roberta gasped.

A pair of thin hands found Gwen's face and cradled it with shaking fingers. Gwen found her sister, wrapped her arms around her, and pulled her out of the bunk bed and into her lap. Roberta said nothing; neither of them did. They just clung to one another, their limbs entwined, two sisters reunited at last.

Chapter Seven

Gwen opened the door as quietly as she could. Despite the fact that lack of sleep made her eyelids feel heavy and itchy, her heart was pounding with excitement – and not just because she was going to see Roberta in just a few precious minutes.

For just over a week, Gwen had been sneaking out of the dormitory almost every night to see her sister. And every night, Nick was there, waiting for her, just as he was now at the end of the passage. He didn't carry a candle; light would only give them away. Instead, he stood right where the single patch of moonlight from the tiny, grimy window fell upon him. Something about its soft, silvery touch on his features made them seem more handsome than ever; its light reflected in his eyes made them somehow even deeper, even darker.

Gwen couldn't tear her eyes away from them as she quietly shut the door behind her. He smiled at her, holding out a hand, but concern tinged his face when she stepped into the light.

"You're tired," he observed.

"It's worth it," said Gwen. "I have to see Bobbie." *And you*, she added in her heart.

"Do you sleep enough?" asked Nick gently.

Gwen turned her face away. "I would rather be sleeping too little because of slipping out to see my sister, than sleeping too little because of nightmares about her," she said quietly.

Nick's fingers folded around hers. "Let's go, then," he said.

Even in the pitch dark and awful cold of the workhouse, with its austere walls rising up around them, Gwen felt more hopeful than ever when Nick was holding her hand. It felt like he was a guiding light; she needed no candle or lantern to lead the way when Nick was with her.

Before long, they had made the familiar turn through the echoing space of the dining hall, and they were walking up the hallway to the girls' dormitory. Nick stopped at the corner of the hall. "I'll keep watch," he whispered. "Try to be quick."

"I will." Gwen squeezed his fingers. "Thank you, Nick." She paused. "I know you're taking a risk by helping me."

"You..." Nick stopped, as though struggling to find words. "You're worth it," he said at last.

Gwen had never felt worth anything before, and it made goosebumps rise on her arms to hear it. She hardly knew what to do with the feelings rising in her chest, so she let go of Nick's hand and turned away, feeling her way along the wall to the dormitory door.

Somehow, Roberta had managed to move herself to the bunk right by the door. As soon as Gwen pushed it open, she heard the rustle of movement in Roberta's bunk. She smiled with happy anticipation. In just a few seconds, she would have Roberta in her arms…

Brilliant light filled the hallway, making Gwen spin around. "I've caught you, you foolish child!" roared a voice of triumph.

Gwen had just enough presence of mind to slam the door shut before Mrs. Webb was upon her. The towering presence of the matron eclipsed her vision; Mrs. Webb's eyes were blazing with anger. She seized the front of Gwen's dress and hauled her closer until they were nose to nose. "I knew someone was sneaking through these halls," she hissed.

Gwen felt ice cold, not only for herself, but for Nick. She forced herself not to look towards where he was standing. Maybe he could still get away if she kept Mrs. Webb's attention on her.

"Please, ma'am, I..." she began.

"You can give no explanation that will excuse your absolute impudence, you horrible child," snapped Mrs. Webb. "You know the rules. You are not permitted to leave your dormitory except to the lavatory. It is a simple rule!"

Gwen felt tears of terror stinging her eyes, but her body trembled with determination. She had to keep Mrs. Webb away from Roberta and Nick.

"I'm sorry, ma'am. I'm sorry," she babbled. "I just... I was..."

The door creaked, and someone stepped out beside Gwen. Her heart froze. *No, Bobbie, no!*

But it wasn't Roberta's voice that spoke. It was June's.

"Did you catch her, ma'am?" she asked in her prim little tone.

Gwen felt a wave of anger engulf her. In that moment, she would gladly have slapped June.

"Yes, thank you, June," said Mrs. Webb, her tone a little less irritable. She glared at Gwen. "I don't suppose you're going to tell me why you keep coming to this dormitory, are you? Or who helps you to get here? Is it that sister of yours?"

"No, ma'am!" The lie sprang easily to her lips, born of sheer desperation. "She has nothing to do with it."

"Ha! I'm sure," growled Mrs. Webb. She switched her grip from the front of Gwen's dress to her ear. "You're coming with me, child. June, go back to bed."

She strode off, sending pangs of burning pain through Gwen's ear, and Gwen stumbled after her, yelping with ignored agony. The last thing she saw, as they turned down the hallway toward the refractory ward, was June's face.

It was utterly smug.

~ ~ ~ ~ ~

Gwen had never seen the refractory ward before, but she'd heard the stories from some of the other girls who had not been so lucky. They were stories of loneliness and darkness, of inexpressible cold and fear.

And none of them had done the real refractory ward justice.

When Mrs. Webb pushed the door open, Gwen could hardly believe how tiny the room was. There was a sleeping pallet that ran down the entire length of one wall; it was not quite long enough that a grown woman would be able to stretch out on it. A bucket stood beside it, and that was all. It was no more than five feet long and maybe three feet wide.

And there were no windows.

"Ma'am, please!" Gwen cried, gripped with indescribable fear.

Mrs. Webb shoved her into the room with wrenching pain on her ear. "You brought this on your own head, child," she spat.

The door slammed, and Gwen was sealed in total darkness. For a few panicked seconds, she tried to breathe deeply, to tell herself that there was no real danger. But the attempt did not last long. The darkness enfolded her, rushed into her lungs with every breath, stifled her. She flung herself against the door and screamed, pounding her fists upon the wood until they were raw, until her voice was raw, until her entire being felt raw.

Then she slid to the ground, her face pressed against the door, and sobbed with whatever strength she had left.

~ ~ ~ ~ ~

When Mrs. Webb finally removed Gwen from the refractory ward, she had been surprised to find out that she was only confined there for two nights and a day.

It was just after breakfast that Mrs. Webb had come to get her. She found herself wishing the matron could have brought her out before breakfast instead; they had given her food while she was in the ward, half rations of stale bread and cold gruel, but she had had no appetite for it. Her throat had been too sore from crying, her heart too shattered by the darkness and loneliness.

As Mrs. Webb had led her to the laundry, though, Gwen had regretted it.

It was just before lunch now, and Gwen had been toiling away at the washing tub for what felt like forever. Her stomach burned with hunger, sending pangs up through her back and shoulders as she bent over the scalding tub and rubbed a piece of threadbare, striped clothing in her chapped hands. Bend, scrub, scrub, straighten, toss the clothing into the rinse tub, bend again, scrub again. Her body ached from the monotony of it, but it was better than the refractory ward, even if the crush of women around the tub was stifling at times.

At last, the bell rang for lunchtime. Gwen straightened up, relief washing over her. She finished scrubbing the last piece of laundry — to leave work unfinished would be to subject herself to even more punishment – and threw it into the rinse water to wait until after lunch. The women all turned to file out of the hot, stifling room, and as always, Gwen found herself jostled to the very back of the line, with the other younger girls. None of them spoke to her. No one ever did; sometimes not even when she asked them if they had ever known her mother.

She was the last one through the door, and she turned around to close it, and that was when she spotted him. Nick was standing against the corner in the shadows, and he startled her a little. She jumped back, stifling a yelp.

"Please!" Nick whispered, holding out a hand as he glanced at the last few girls. "Don't be alarmed. I... I just wanted to apologize."

His eyes were deep with shame, and refused to meet her own; he looked down at his shoes instead.

"Apologize?" said Gwen.

"For letting the matron catch you." Nick's voice trembled. "She came from the other side... I was expecting her to come, if she came, from her chambers. I was looking the wrong way. By the time she came around the corner, I didn't know what to do. I should have called out. I should have stopped her, or... or..."

"I'm not angry, Nick," said Gwen softly.

He looked up at her then, his face shocked. "You're not?"

She had been, a few times, during the long and awful hours in the refractory ward. But she had realized at last that there was no point. Why push away the one person who had been her ally, no matter what his mistake had cost her?

"No," she said quietly. "I'm not. What good would it have done if you had tried to stop Mrs. Webb, anyway? You would only have been punished." She paused, taking a deep, shaky breath. "Nick... do you know what happened to Roberta?"

"She's all right," said Nick, giving her a quick smile. "Mrs. Webb couldn't put her in the refractory ward since you were already in there. I talked her into just halving her rations for a day."

Gwen's heart squeezed at the thought of Roberta's pitiful rations being halved, but she was still grateful; it could have been so much worse. "Thank you," she whispered.

Nick reached towards her as though he would have laid his hand on her shoulder, then let it fall down by his side again instead.

"Are you going to try again?" he said softly.

She turned her face away. "It doesn't matter," she said. "I don't want to get you in trouble."

"So you *are* going to try again, and you don't want my help, because you're afraid of what Mrs. Webb will do to me," said Nick.

His words were utterly true. Gwen said nothing.

"Please, Gwen." Nick touched her arm. "Is it a good idea? Won't Roberta just be punished again if you're caught?"

The thought had occurred to Gwen before, too, and now it gripped her throat with tears. She looked up at him, fighting to squeeze out the words.

"I don't have a choice," she said. "I can't just leave Roberta. I'm all she has, Nick. No punishment could be worse than total separation." She hung her head, hot tears splashing down her cheeks. "For both of us."

"All right, then." Nick hesitated. "But then I'm going to keep on helping you."

"No. You don't have to do this. I don't want you to get in trouble," said Gwen. "Roberta has told me over and over that seeing me at night is the only real joy she has. For her, the risk is worth the reward. But not for you."

Nick reached towards her again, and this time he took her hand, folding his warm fingers around it.

"That's not true," he said softly.

~ ~ ~ ~ ~

Gwen's heart pounded against her ribs as she hurried through the dark hallways of the silent workhouse. Her sweaty feet stuck to the floor, making the sensation unpleasant, like grime was sticking to the soles of her feet. Here, in the hallway between the dining hall and the dormitory, it was absolutely dark.

The perfect darkness reminded her appallingly of the refractory ward. In fact, she felt she might have turned and fled straight back into her own dormitory if she had to face that darkness alone; it was too terrifying, too much like those awful hours in that dark room. But there was one key difference, and that was the feeling of Nick's hand wrapped around her own. It was warmth and light to her in that dark place.

Soon they turned the corner and saw the sliver of moonlight shining on the bare floor, and Nick squeezed her hand. "I'll stand by the door this time," he whispered. "That way I can keep better watch up and down the hall."

"But you'll have nowhere to hide if the matron comes," said Gwen.

"Don't worry. Come on," said Nick. "We don't have much time."

Gwen swallowed hard, forcing herself to let go of his hand as they reached the dormitory door. She grasped the handle, pushed it open slowly, and felt all of her fears fade as she peered into the dormitory. June wouldn't be expecting her. Everyone would think that her stay in the refractory ward had warned her off trying to see Roberta again. She was going to get away with it.

She tiptoed over to Roberta's bunk. "Bobbie?" she whispered.

Roberta stirred, sitting up suddenly. Gwen couldn't quite see her face; she just made out a vague outline of her sister in the dark.

"Gwen!" she gasped, and small, thin hands grabbed at Gwen's arms. Gwen felt tears of relief starting to her eyes. She wrapped her arms around Roberta, sinking to the ground with her sister cradled in her lap, her face buried in Roberta's neck. Roberta was sobbing, holding onto her with all of her strength.

"It's all right, Bobbie," Gwen whispered. "It's all right. I'm here."

"I was afraid you'd never come again," Roberta whispered. "I was afraid you'd left me."

Gwen tightened her grip around her sister's thin body. "I will never leave you," she said. "Never."

Suddenly, the door swung open. Gwen jumped, but the thin figure silhouetted in the doorway belonged to Nick.

"Gwen!" he hissed. "Hide!"

"What?" Gwen gasped.

Before he could respond, the room was suddenly flooded with light. It was piercing and sharp, stabbing right into Gwen's eyes so brilliantly that she cried out in pain.

"No!" Nick cried.

"Here they are, Mrs. Webb!" trilled June's hateful little voice. "I told you she'd come back."

Slowly, trembling with horror, clutching Roberta's stiff body in her arms, Gwen looked up. Mrs. Webb strode into the dormitory, brilliantly lit by the gas lamps in its ceiling. She looked more towering and more irate than ever; her eyes were red from lack of sleep, and heightened the effect of rage pouring out of every inch of her.

"You were right after all, June," hissed Mrs. Webb, glaring down at Gwen. "I thought not even Gwendoline would be stupid enough to come back here after her time in the refractory ward."

Gwen swallowed the tears of terror that filled her throat. "Please, ma'am..." she began, getting to her feet and shoving Roberta away, desperate to draw all of the attention to her.

Mrs. Webb moved quickly. Her hand flashed out, seizing Roberta's arm with a force that made the girl squeal.

"No! Bobbie!" Gwen shrieked.

"Gwen!" screamed Roberta.

"Silence!" roared Mrs. Webb. She grabbed Gwen's ear in hard, unyielding fingers; Gwen heard the faint tear of skin and felt pain bloom across the base of her ear. Yelping, she allowed her head to be forced downwards.

Mrs. Webb raised her voice. "Look at this, children!" she shouted. "Do you see what will happen if you break my rules? Do you see what will be done to you if you sneak around my workhouse at night?"

The dormitory was filled with a terrified silence. From her awkward position, Gwen could just see

June where she stood a few feet away. Her arms were folded, and she didn't bother to hide her smirk.

"Come with me," snapped Mrs. Webb, turning around and storming out of the doorway.

Nick was standing in the hall, round-eyed, his face very pale. "Ma'am, where are you taking them?" he gasped.

Roberta was sobbing, not bothering to try to pull her arm out of Mrs. Webb's grip. Gwen could feel a trickle of blood against her skin; she panted, struggling to keep up with Mrs. Webb, her back and neck aching from the awkward way they were twisted around.

Mrs. Webb ignored Nick completely. She was walking away from the dining hall, towards a hallway that Gwen knew very well: the hallway she had always mopped when she wanted to talk to Nick.

It felt as though her veins had been filled with ice. Mrs. Webb was taking them towards the front door.

"Please, ma'am," she begged, "don't do this. Oh, please, please, throw me in the refractory ward, take away our food, but please…"

"Clearly the usual punishments have no effect on children as bad, sinful and disobedient as you two," spat Mrs. Webb.

They had reached the front door. Mrs. Webb released them both; Roberta collapsed to the ground, sobbing. Gwen fell to her knees, hurt and terrified. She put an arm around Roberta as Mrs. Webb took a huge keyring out of her pocket and unlocked the front door.

"Please," Gwen begged.

"You've brought this on yourselves," spat Mrs. Webb.

She kicked the door open, and a blast of cold air hissed into the workhouse. Gwen stared out at the front courtyard, at the palisades that looked like they were impaling the night sky.

"Get up and walk," said Mrs. Webb.

Her tone held a terrifying warning. Gwen hauled herself to her feet, pulling Roberta up with her. She didn't dare to look back at Nick, who was still behind them. Instead, she walked out into the cool autumn night, feeling the icy kiss of the wind on her cheeks, the dampness in the air and on the muddy ground as they walked across the courtyard to the gate.

Mrs. Webb unlocked it and pushed it wide. "Go," she said.

"No! No, no, no, no!" shrieked Roberta, throwing herself backwards against Gwen's arm. "No!"

Gwen knew that resistance would be useless. Blinded by tears, she turned to Mrs. Webb and made one last attempt at appealing to the matron.

"Ma'am, we'll die out there," she whispered. "Please, don't send Roberta away. It's not her fault."

"No, it's not," said Mrs. Webb icily. "It's yours."

She placed a flat hand on Gwen's shoulder and shoved her out into the dark street. Gwen tripped over the curb and fell backwards, landing with an icy splash in the gutter. She gasped with pain and shock.

"No!" Nick lunged forward. "Please, Mrs. Webb." He turned to her, tears running down his cheeks. "Don't send them away. You know they won't survive."

Mrs. Webb's eyes narrowed. "You lied to me, Nicholas," she said.

"No!" Gwen gasped, scrambling to her feet, her wet dress clinging to her body. "No, he did nothing wrong!"

Nicholas met her eyes. "Yes," he said quietly. "I lied to you because what you're doing is wrong. You can't separate families like this."

Mrs. Webb was trembling with rage. "After everything I've done for you," she spat. "How could you betray me like this?"

"I believed in you, Mrs. Webb. You were so kind to me and to so many others when I was younger," said Nick. "What happened? How can you even think of throwing two helpless children onto the street?"

"How dare you speak to me in that way!" shrieked Mrs. Webb.

"Please." Nick laid his hands on her shoulders, his voice breaking. "Just tell me what happened. Why are you like this now?"

Mrs. Webb's face crumpled. She turned away, shaking off his hands.

"If one sees enough suffering, one has a choice," she said, her voice low and harsh. "You can allow it to break you, or allow it to harden you." She raised her chin, her eyes meeting Nick's. "Goodbye, Nicholas."

He stared at her. "Goodbye?"

"Yes. Never come back here again." Mrs. Webb turned away. "Ever."

"No! Don't!" screamed Gwen.

Nick stepped through the gate and took her hand, raising a finger to her lips to silence her. "It's no use, Gwen," he said. "She's made up her mind."

Mrs. Webb slammed the gate and walked back into the workhouse. She pulled the door closed behind her with a quiet click, leaving the children alone in the dark street.

Roberta looked up at Nick, her eyes red with tears. "What are we going to do now, Nicholas?" she whispered.

Nick closed his hand a little more firmly on Gwen's.

"Whatever we have to do to stay alive," he said, his voice trembling.

There were a few moments of silence as they contemplated their appalling predicament. The cold wind chilled Gwen in her wet dress, and she shivered, wrapping her arms around herself. She and Roberta had been unable to survive out here even with Mama's help. How much less would they survive now?

"There's nothing left for us here," said Nick. "Come on."

He tugged her forward, and they stepped into the cold and silent city.

Part Three

THE WAIF'S LOST FAMILY

Chapter Eight

One Year Later

Gwen tried to make her glance down the street look nonchalant. Truth be told, it was easy enough to blend into the crowd here. This street just a few blocks from the warehouse district was always busy, especially at this time of morning, and a crush of Londoners from all walks of life filled the sidewalk from edge to edge. There were some ladies and gentlemen who wore well-cut clothes and bits of fine jewellery; others were tradespeople in work-worn clothing with well-scrubbed faces and toolboxes in their hands; but the majority looked more like Gwen. They were factory workers and homeless people, shuffling along the road of life with the same lack of enthusiasm with which they trod the weary miles to work, their eyes glassily staring into nothing, their faces pale and unwashed.

In her ragged dress, Gwen blended in well enough where she leaned against a lamppost, pretending to be resting from her walk. She ran her hands over the fabric, drying the sweat on her palms. This dress was paper-thin to the touch, but she knew that keeping her workhouse dress on would have meant she would be turned in for stealing — a fact that Mrs. Webb had been too angry to remember when she'd thrown Gwen, Roberta and Nick onto the streets. She had scavenged this one from a garbage can and patched it as well as she could.

Lifting her eyes, she spotted Roberta hiding in the shadowed doorway of an abandoned shop. Roberta's keen eyes were flashing through the crowd. Despite her ragged clothes, she stood with her shoulders back, chin up; and despite the hunger that had plagued their lives in the year since leaving the workhouse, Roberta was now taller than Gwen. There was something fierce in her eyes, too, something that had startled Gwen the first time she saw it, but there was no doubt that that strength had helped them all survive the winter.

Gwen saw Roberta straighten slightly, her eyes locked on something – or rather, someone. She followed Roberta's gaze into the crowd and immediately spotted the target. It was a paunchy, balding, middle-aged man; he wore spectacles, and even as the crowd jostled him, he was looking down at the newspaper in his hands. And she could just see the flash of something metal protruding from the pocket of his lapel. A cigar case, a flask – it didn't matter. It would be worth something at the local pawnshop.

Gwen felt her stomach tighten with fear and disgust. She hated what was going to happen next, but she had no choice.

Roberta had stepped out of the doorway and was walking with the crowd, head down, towards the paunchy man, her hands in her pockets. Gwen took a deep breath. She glanced over her shoulder and saw Nick striding towards her. His tousled hair hung over his eyes, smears of grime on his cheeks; between that and his out-at-the-elbows coat and gap-fronted boots, he looked every inch a disreputable character. Nonetheless, there was a smile in his eyes as they sparkled at Gwen.

"Oi, woman!" he shouted, and Gwen had to stifle a laugh. Today, he'd chosen an outrageous country accent that sounded nothing like his normal voice.

"What do you think you're doing, wandering around out here on your own?"

Gwen knew her line well. She turned to face him, stepping deliberately into the flow of foot traffic. "I'm doing as I please, thank you very much!" she cried. "You can't tell me what to do, Finley!"

"I expected you back home with the groceries an hour ago!" shouted Nick. "What are you doing, lollygagging about on the streets like this? It's the shopkeeper over yonder, isn't it? He's caught your eye, has he?"

Gwen tossed her head. "And what business of yours is it if he has?" she demanded.

Her eyes slid sideways as she spoke. A crush of pedestrians was building up around them as they tried to squeeze awkwardly past her. Several were staring at her goggle-eyed for her audacity. Gwen knew their little act was ridiculous, but it certainly did what it was designed to do – it drew attention.

The paunchy man was among the stuttering crowd. And Roberta, her head still down, was slipping towards him through the people like a fish through water.

Gwen quickly pulled her eyes away. Nick was in the midst of his angry speech about her impudence and flippancy, and she tossed her head, planting her hands on her hips.

"Well, don't just stand there!" Nick roared. "Go and get those groceries!"

"Fine!" Gwen snorted and turned away, marching off in a random direction. Her heart stung every time they went through this routine. Not because of Nick's raised tone; she knew that was all a game, and it was something precious between them — but because she wished she could simply walk off and buy groceries. Then they wouldn't have to do this charade, or what always followed.

A few moments later, the three of them regrouped in an alley running behind the row of shops. It was deserted, as usual for this time of day, except for a few huge rats that scuttled and squeaked in the shadows.

"Well done, Gwen," panted Nick, who had run there around the block. "I thought you were extra cheeky today." His smile somehow made Gwen feel a little better about what she'd done.

She turned to Roberta. "Did you get it?" she asked.

Roberta's eyes sparkled with mischief. "I did!" she said triumphantly, reaching into her pocket and pulling out a silver cigar case. It flashed in the sun, but only briefly before she tucked it away again before anyone else could see it.

"Bravo!" Nick laughed. "Who would have thought that that frightened little girl would make such an excellent pickpocket?"

"Certainly not me," said Gwen.

"Well, I'm glad I can be helpful." Roberta laughed, her new confidence shining in her eyes. "Come on – let's pawn this. I'm starving."

Gwen wasn't surprised. Despite the jovial mood that Roberta and Nick always managed to pull together after a pickpocketing session went well, she knew they both felt as weak and shaky as she did. It had been two days since any of them had eaten.

And that was why she said nothing about the black weight resting on her chest, a weight that only grew with every trinket or fistful of coins they stole from the pockets of unwary pedestrians.

She had never thought she would stoop to stealing. But as she had learned years ago while Teddy was ill, when the choice was between theft or death, theft won every time.

~ ~ ~ ~ ~

The abandoned warehouse was even colder than the workhouse had been, but at least the top floor of it had only a few rats, and most of the windows had been boarded up. A thin draft still blew through the gaps between the boards in the windows, whistling in a steady and melancholy wail around the few furnishings that Gwen, Nick and Roberta called their own: an old, leaky bucket in which a fire made from a few damp coals burned faintly; four old flour sacks that served as two mattresses; two ancient, tattered blankets. That was all that they had. It looked more pitiful than ever with the faint firelight flickering over it.

Gwen sat on a broken crate by the one window that was not boarded up. It was cold here, but bearable in early summer, and sitting by the window looking out over the lights of London far below was better than lying by the fire and listening to Roberta's snoring when she couldn't sleep.

She leaned her cheek against the rough windowpane and gazed out at the thousand squares and pinpricks of light. The day had been windy, and it was one of the clearest nights Gwen had ever seen. It was almost impossible to tell where the city ended and the stars began.

She wondered if Mama was out there somewhere. Had she escaped the workhouse somehow too? Or was she still there? Or perhaps her soul had been set free from the grubby yellow of the city lights down below, and soared now among the silvery stars. Tears filled her eyes at the thought.

"Can't sleep?" said Nick softly.

Gwen looked up. He had come over to the window, and he leaned his elbows on it; the wind ruffled the dark tousles of his hair.

"Did you have enough to eat?" he asked, looking down at her. His eyes were wreathed in shadow, and unreadable.

"Oh, yes, thank you," said Gwen. For once, she spoke the truth: they had been lucky, and found a baker about to throw away his stale bread. They had all eaten their fill tonight.

"So what's keeping you up?" Nick asked. His voice was gentle.

Gwen sighed, propping her chin on her elbow.

"You grew up being taught in the workhouse chapel," she said quietly. "You know that what we're doing is wrong."

Nick was silent for a long moment, looking out over the city.

"I don't see that we have a choice, Gwen," he said, his tone calm.

"I know we don't. I would do anything to see Roberta healthy – and you," said Gwen. "But doesn't it ever bother you?"

Nick sighed. "Yes," he admitted. "It keeps me up sometimes, too. I know that many times we only take trinkets from the rich, but that doesn't mean it's not stealing." He paused. "And today... that cigar case had an inscription on it when I took it to the pawn broker. It was from that man's daughter."

Gwen's heart felt squeezed.

"I think that cigar case meant something to him, but not as much as eating for the first time in days meant to us," said Nick.

"You're right." Gwen ran a hand through her matted hair. "Oh, Nick, I know you're right. I just wish that someday we could survive without having to do such things. Without having to go into a workhouse and get separated from our families. Without having to work in factories that murder us. Without having…" She sucked in a breath, then let it out slowly. "Without having to beg."

Nick knew what had happened to Teddy. His hand found hers in the dark, and squeezed it.

"One day we will," he said softly. "We'll have a safe home and a happy family and enough food to go around."

Gwen returned the squeeze. She knew Nick was only saying it to make her feel better, but when he spoke of such things – of happiness and safety – it made them seem so much more real.

"Nick…" she said.

"Yes?"

Gwen fell silent. She didn't know how to tell him what was on her heart: that he was the guiding light in her dark and silent world.

~ ~ ~ ~ ~

The policeman on the street corner was making Gwen nervous.

His brass buttons shone in the summer light; the clear night had turned into a beautiful day. Normally, Gwen would be enjoying the sun on her face, but she found herself incapable of dragging her eyes away from the policeman.

He was a tall man, imposing, his back ramrod-straight, his hat pulled down low over his eyes as they travelled up and down the busy street. A truncheon hung at his hip, an ugly black thing that looked heavy and mean. Gwen tried not to imagine it smashing down onto her skull.

"We should go somewhere else," she whispered to Nick as they walked up the street, hand-in-hand. They never repeated the same act twice in a row; it would draw too much suspicion.

"Why? Because of the bobby?" Nick shrugged. "We'll draw his attention just like all the others."

"I don't like it," said Gwen. "It's too dangerous."

Nick squeezed her hand. "Look at that old gentleman, Gwen," he said urgently. "That's a *gold* chain hanging from his pocket. It could feed us for weeks."

Gwen unwillingly let her eyes slide in the direction of their target again. He was an elderly gentleman, balding, with jolly red cheeks; he looked like Father Christmas, and the thought of robbing him sat uneasily in Gwen's stomach even without the tension caused by that policeman. Still, she knew that Nick was right. The chain swung tantalizingly from the gentleman's pocket as he strolled down the street, digging a silver-headed cane into the sidewalk with every jaunty step.

She had to hurt that gentleman to feed her sister. And if the choice was between her darling Roberta and a stranger, it was no choice at all.

"Ready?" whispered Nick.

"Ready." Gwen swallowed hard and gripped his hand tightly.

"Let's go," whispered Nick.

They turned together; Gwen glanced up and down the street, and finding it free of traffic, they began to stroll across it. She made sure to walk carelessly, legs swinging as though the street was neatly paved instead of having slippery, rounded cobblestones – the whole reason they had chosen this street for this particular distraction.

"Where would you like to go next, darling?" Nick asked her, giving her a wide, false smile.

Gwen gave an unladylike giggle. "Let's try the slop-shop," she said. "I'm sure they'll have a wedding suit for you."

Even though the words were nothing but pretend, they made her heart flip over in her chest, and for a moment she forgot what they were doing; she smiled up into Nick's soft eyes, and imagined him in a real wedding suit on a real wedding day...

He squeezed her hand sharply, and she realized that they had nearly reached the sidewalk. Just in time, Gwen skidded her left foot across the cobbles. "Oh!" she cried dramatically, snatching at Nick's hands.

He flailed at her, but allowed her fingers to slip through his. "Darling!" he cried.

Gwen crashed to the ground a little harder than she had planned. Her knee stung sharply, lending some sincerity to her voice as she cried out. "Oh! Oh! My ankle!" she shrieked, grabbing at her ankle.

With her head hung low, her matted hair was falling into her eyes; she glanced up through it, and saw that it was working. People were stopping on the street to gawk at her as she gave another dramatic howl and clutched her uninjured foot with both hands. Nick was gasping and fluttering around her uselessly; even the policeman was leaning forward, watching them.

Out of the corner of her eye, she saw Roberta hurrying down the sidewalk, head down, hands in her pockets. The gentleman stood a few yards from her, staring at Gwen with concern in his eyes.

She ducked her head again. "I think it's broken!" she wailed.

"Oh, darling!" whimpered Nick. "Oh, help us, help us!"

"Stop!" roared a male voice.

Gwen sat up, horror rippling through her, and saw her worst nightmare playing out before her eyes. The jolly-faced gentleman's happy expression had vanished; his eyes were wide and cold now, and he held his walking stick above his head, brandished like a blade. And in his other hand, his knuckles white, he gripped Roberta's wrist. Her fingers still lingered in his lapel pocket.

"Stop thief!" bellowed the old gentleman, raising his stick a little higher.

"Police! Police!" cried one of the onlookers, a young woman, clutching her children closer to her. "Help! Help him!"

"No!" shrieked Roberta, twisting, her face a mask of terror as she tried to wrest her hand from the gentleman's grip.

In a flash, Nick had yanked Gwen to her feet. "Run!" he cried. "We've got to run!"

But Gwen couldn't run, not with Roberta struggling and yanking at the old gentleman's arm like a fish on the line, fighting for her life. The policeman's whistle was blowing; he was running down the sidewalk, his hand on his truncheon.

"Bobbie!" Gwen shrieked, the war cry tearing loose from her lips. She yanked her hand from Nick's grip and threw herself onto the sidewalk, her hands extended, twisted into claws of fury as she rushed down upon the old gentleman.

It was a split second too late. The old man's walking cane whistled through the air and smashed down onto Roberta's temple. Blood bloomed across her pale skin, and she crumpled to the ground with a yelp of pain.

"No!" yelled Gwen. The old gentleman had his stick raised again, and she flung herself against him, her hands clawing at the arm that held the stick. He let out an astonished cry. Her momentum bore them both off their feet, and they fell to the pavement, her elbow smacking painfully against the stone.

"Gwen!" cried Roberta in dismay.

The gentleman's hand seized her hair; Gwen twisted, feeling it rip from her scalp as she rolled out of his grip. He lunged at her, his face twisted with rage, lips pulled back over snarling teeth. Gwen scrambled to her feet, rushing to where Roberta had a hand clasped to her head. The policeman was almost upon them, ringing his bell wildly, summoning more. She grabbed Roberta's arm.

"Run!" she shrieked.

Roberta stumbled to her feet, and Gwen bolted, dragging her sister behind them. The policeman's whistle pursued them down the street; people were stopping to stare, and Gwen pushed them aside, ignoring their cries of surprise and pain. Roberta was sobbing; Gwen had no time to look back at her. She just hauled her sister along with her, and they ran for their lives.

"Here!" shouted a blessedly familiar voice.

Gwen looked to her left. Nick was standing at the mouth of an alleyway across the street, beckoning wildly.

"Come on!" she cried, jerking at Roberta's hand. They turned and dashed across the street, heedless of the traffic hissing this way and that; drivers shouted curses, hooves resounded around them, but they made it to the other side somehow and plunged down the alley with Nick close behind them.

Gwen glanced back as they ran. There was no sign of the policeman or the old gentleman; Robert's breathing came in shallow gasps of pain.

"We need to stop, Nick," she gasped.

"Here!" Nick dived down another little alley and pushed open a rickety gate. They stumbled into a courtyard of sorts; there were garbage cans and shapeless, lumpy sacks lying everywhere. Nick dived behind one of the cans, and Gwen and Roberta collapsed beside him. Roberta's hand was still pressed to her head. Blood seeped between her fingers, startling red against the dirty skin.

"Shhh. Shhh," whispered Gwen, terrified. She wrapped an arm around her sister and held her close. "Hush now."

"They're coming," whispered Nick.

Gwen held her breath. Roberta was trembling uncontrollably, her thin shoulders jerking against Gwen's arm. She stroked her hair. Loud footsteps were coming down the alley, getting closer and closer.

They stopped not far away, and a gruff masculine voice spoke. Roberta gave a tiny whimper of fear.

"I think they went this way," it said.

"Maybe we should split up. One of us can take this road, the other, this one," said another.

"No, no. There's a young man with them. We might end up in a fight," said the first. "Let's both go this way. We can come back if we don't find anything."

"All right," agreed the first.

Their feet began to run again, and Gwen cowered down against Nick, too afraid to move. But the men had chosen to continue down the alley. Their thudding footsteps receded into the distance, and Gwen's breath came out in a rush. She leaned back against the wall, Roberta sobbing on her shoulder, pain shooting up her exhausted limbs.

Nick got to his feet. "Come on," he said, his voice hollow and scared. He grabbed Roberta's arm and pulled it over his shoulders. "We can't stay here."

Propping Roberta up between them, they stumbled out of the alley and toward the abandoned warehouse that was their only home.

Chapter Nine

Roberta's face was very pale. She lay curled on her side on the tattered blanket that separated her goose-pimpled flesh from the cold floor of the warehouse, her head pillowed only on her folded hands. Gwen had done her best to clean the ugly wound on her head; her forehead was a mass of black bruising and dried blood. She leaned over and brushed some of Roberta's hair out of the wound. Her sister's face crinkled in pain for an instant; she let out a soft moan, then went back to sleep.

"Hush, Bobbie dear," whispered Gwen, stroking Roberta's hair. "Just sleep."

There were footsteps on the staircase, and Gwen tensed, but the figure that climbed up onto their floor was Nick's. He carried an armful of old sticks that he had stolen somewhere for firewood. Crouching down, he laid them on the fire, wincing when it guttered from the dampness of the stolen wood.

"How is she?" he asked Gwen in a whisper, glancing over at Roberta.

"It's very sore." Gwen sighed. "But at least she's gone to sleep now. I hope that's a good thing."

"I'm sure it is," said Nick. He sat down beside her, leaning over to look at the wound, and flinched. "We have to keep that clean."

"I'm so afraid it will get infected," said Gwen, her voice wobbling.

"It won't." Nick put an arm around her shoulders.

She leaned against him, but this time, his reassurance was difficult to believe. She tipped back her chin to look up at him. "You don't know that," she whispered. "Nick, I..." Her throat tightened. "I can't lose her," she whispered.

His arm tightened around her, but he didn't say anything. Gwen leaned her head against his shoulder. "I think we should go back to the workhouse," she whispered.

Nick pulled back, shocked, and looked down at her. "What?" he said.

"I know it was hard there, Nick," she said, "but what else can we do?" She shook her head. "We can't go on like this. And what if Roberta gets sick?"

Nick let out a long breath. "I know you don't like stealing..." he began.

"It's not just that," said Gwen. "Look at her, Nick. What are we going to do to help her? In the workhouse, at least a doctor would do *something* for her. Even if he only had something she could take for the pain."

There was a beat of silence. They both stared down at Roberta's pale face, listening to her shallow, ragged breathing.

"And maybe..." Gwen sighed. "Maybe we could find our mama. Maybe she's still in there."

"You'd be separated from Bobbie again," said Nick softly.

"It's better than watching her..." Gwen closed her eyes tight against the tears, remembering the way Teddy's tiny body had fought for each breath. "It's better than watching her die," she whispered.

The silence grew again. Nick squeezed her tightly against him.

"All right," he said. "I don't think they'll take us back, but you're right. We've got to try." He held her a little closer. "We'll go in the morning."

She looked up at him. "Thank you," she whispered.

He leaned down then, and pressed his lips with startling tenderness to her forehead. Then he got up, leaving her on the floor, a little dazed by the unexpected perfection of his kiss to her forehead.

"I'm going to find some food," he said, and was gone.

Gwen reached up to touch her head, as if she could still feel the burning warmth of his kiss on her skin. And a tiny spark of hope began to glow softly in her heart.

~ ~ ~ ~ ~

Roberta's head looked no better the next day. The blue and purple mess of bruising only seemed to have grown overnight, and she walked carefully, as though the slightest trip or bump would cause her pain. Squinting against the sun, she was very quiet as they headed up the street.

"Maybe you should take Roberta back, Gwen," said Nick, looking over at her. "We still have an entire block to walk. And what if we have to turn back? What if they won't take us?"

"I hope they don't," said Roberta, speaking the words carefully as though they caused her pain. "I don't want to go back there."

Gwen sighed, squeezing Roberta's arm, which was threaded through hers. "I know you don't, Bobbie," she said. "But look at you. Your poor head..." She took a deep breath. "Even the workhouse was better than starving out here. Maybe we'll even find Mama."

Roberta gave her a surly look, but it was clear that she was hurting too much to say anything more. Gwen tried to still her shaking hands by stroking Roberta's arm gently. In just a few minutes, her sister would be torn from her arms again, and she didn't know when she would see Nick again… but anything, even that, was better than watching Roberta get slowly sicker.

At last, they had made the last turn, and the familiar sight of the street running past the front of the workhouse greeted them. Nick sucked in a sharp breath, and it was all Gwen could do not to do the same. The air here was thick with bad memories, and Gwen found herself wavering, too.

The workhouse had grown in the year since they had been thrown out of it. There were new yards down one side, fenced with iron bars tipped with spikes; through them, Gwen could see women sitting hunched on the concrete, unwinding spools of hard old rope. Picking oakum, it was called, and Gwen knew from the other women's conversations back in the workhouse that there was no harder labour.

That could be her labour, she knew, this very afternoon, if she went on with her plan.

She hesitated. "I don't know about this," she said.

Nick stopped. Roberta stumbled gratefully to a halt beside Gwen, pressing a hand to her forehead with a quiet whimper of pain.

"Do you want to turn back?" he asked Gwen.

Gwen stared down at Roberta, then at Nick, everything inside her trembling. She didn't know what to do. Once again, she held her family's life in her hands, and she didn't know what to do.

"I don't know," she said, tears filling her eyes. "I just want everyone to be safe. Why must I make such terrible choices to keep everyone safe?"

"Gwen?" gasped a voice.

Gwen froze. Roberta's head snapped up, the colour draining from her face.

It couldn't be… surely, it couldn't be. But the voice came again, louder this time. "Gwen!" it cried, and stumbling footsteps crossed the concrete towards them.

Gwen spun around, tears filling her eyes. "Mama?" she breathed.

She had almost believed that the voice belonged to an apparition of her own imagination, some desperate conjuring of a mind tortured by hardship. But she was real, coming towards them in the flesh, her poor knees wobbling with every step. An ugly workhouse dress with its jarring stripes hung from her bony frame like sacking. Limping, her breathing harsh and loud with the effort, she looked so much thinner and older and sicker than Gwen remembered.

But she was their mother, alive and real, coming right towards them, and at that moment, she was the loveliest thing that Gwen had ever seen.

"Mama!" screamed Roberta, flinging herself against the bars and pushing her arms through the gaps to hold out her hands to their mother.

"Oh, Bobbie. Oh, Gwen!" Mama stumbled up to them, collapsed against the bars, and seized Roberta's hands in both of her own. "Come here. Come here so that I can see you. Let me touch you!" A bright tear coursed down her cheek, losing itself in the web of wrinkles.

"Mama, I can't believe it's you," Gwen breathed, reaching for one of the gnarled hands.

Mama wrapped work-worn fingers around Gwen's and squeezed them tight. "My dear children," she sobbed. "I thought I'd lost you. It's been so, so long."

\

"Mama, I'm sorry." The words gushed from Gwen at last; it was a glorious relief to speak them aloud. "I'm so sorry for everything that went wrong."

"Gwen!" Mama looked up at her, her eyes still overflowing with tears. "My darling, how can you apologize?"

Gwen's heart thumped hard, swelling against her ribs. What did Mama mean by that? Suddenly she longed for Mama to say the words that would set her free: that it wasn't Gwen's fault that Teddy was dead and Joey was dead and that they had been separated for three years, that none of this had ever been her fault.

"Gwen, darling, it's..." Mama began.

"HEY!" roared a voice from inside the yard. "YOU!"

Mama's head whipped around, and Gwen felt a jolt of terror run through her body at the familiar voice.

It was Mrs. Webb. She came storming across the yard like an oncoming hurricane, and Gwen felt her bones turn to water at the sight. The year had changed Mrs. Webb not one iota; her chin still jutted, her eyes still flashed, and her voice still trembled with malice as she approached.

"Get away from that fence!" she barked.

Mama let go of Gwen's hand immediately. She stumbled backwards, her face pale and transfixed by fear.

"Mama!" screamed Roberta.

Mrs. Webb stomped forward, placing herself between Mama and the girls. Nick grabbed Gwen's hand, protectively pulling her back from the bars. "Come on," he hissed. "Let's go."

"You three!" Mrs. Webb roared. "What are you doing here?"

"What do you think we're doing here?" cried Roberta. She twisted her hand out of Nick's and stepped forward, her chin raised. "We want to see our mama. You have no right to keep her from us!"

"No right?" shouted Mrs. Webb, her face turning scarlet. "No right? I have every right to do as I please!" She jabbed a finger towards Mama, who stood behind her, tears coursing down her cheeks. "Have you forgotten that I'm the one who keeps everyone alive in this place?"

"Bobbie, come away!" Gwen hissed.

"You can't treat her like this," cried Roberta. "Look how thin she is. What are you doing to our mama?"

"I'm caring for her," spat Mrs. Webb. "And what are you doing back here at my gates?" Her eyes rose to Nick's. "Are you coming back to beg for the good work you once had, Nicholas?"

Nick hesitated, and Gwen looked up at him. His eyes flashed to hers, and she saw the fear in them and knew that he was staying quiet only for her sake.

Her heart broke. She couldn't do this to him or Roberta, not when she had just seen how terrible poor Mama looked. To enter that workhouse wouldn't be their salvation, it would be their doom/

"No, he's not," said Gwen, surprised at the force in her own voice. She stepped forward, her hands bunching into fists. "We will never be treated that way again."

Mrs. Webb's eyes flashed. She spun on her heel and strode away, snagging Mama's arm roughly. "Come," she barked. "You know you're not allowed to go near the fence. A night in the refractory ward will teach you a lesson!"

"No!" Roberta shrieked. "Mama! Don't do this to her!"

"We have to go, Bobbie." Gwen grabbed her arm. "Come on. We have to go."

"Mama!" Roberta sobbed, allowing herself to be towed into the street. "Mama!"

Gwen kept her eyes ahead of her, grabbing Nick's hand and pulling Roberta with her.

She knew that if she looked back to see what Mrs. Webb was doing to their mother, then she, like Roberta, wouldn't be able to tear her eyes away.

~ ~ ~ ~ ~

Gwen cradled the tin mug in her hands. The watery fluid inside had cooled; she had nearly forgotten that she was drinking it at all. It was a pale yellow colour, barely retaining the taste or appearance of tea at all.

She leaned her head against the window-frame, allowing the cool summer breeze to wash over her as she stared out over the city lights. Raising the mug to her lips, she took another sip of the pathetic tea. It was bitter, washing nastily over her tonsils, but at least she could fool her body into thinking that there was something in her stomach.

A few feet from her, lying beside the fire, Roberta stirred. There was a whimper of pain, and her hand went to her head.

"Bobbie?" Gwen put down the mug and crouched down beside her sister, laying a hand on her shoulder.

Roberta didn't wake. She turned onto her other side, cradling her head in both of her hands, and continued to sleep.

Gwen tried to still the cold worry that flared violently in the pit of her stomach. She tugged the blanket a little higher over Roberta's shoulders and smoothed down a stray lock of her sister's hair.

"It's going…" she began, but her tears choked her. She wanted so much to tell Roberta that she was going to be all right, but she'd said those words before. She couldn't wring them out of her throat now.

Somehow, Nick still seemed able to say them. He sat up on his blanket on the other side of the fire, his eyes gentle in the flickering light of the flames. "She'll be all right, Gwen," he said softly. "You'll see."

"I don't know," Gwen admitted, stroking Roberta's hair. "She's not well, Nick. You saw how pale she was when we got back from the workhouse. She needs a doctor." She pushed back her sister's hair. "Look at the bruising here, and here. She's in terrible pain."

Nick got up and came to crouch down beside Gwen. He grimaced when she showed him the bruising that had been hidden under Roberta's hair. "Ah, that must hurt so much," he said.

"I know we did the right thing by not going back into the workhouse," said Gwen. "You were right. We would only have been separated, and Mrs. Webb wouldn't have given Roberta help any more than she's helped our mama…" The thought of Mama made tears sting her eyes again, and she had to pause for a long moment to regain control over her voice.

"Hush, Gwen." Nick rested a hand on her shoulder. "We'll be all right."

"No, we won't." Gwen looked up at him. "What are we going to do, Nick? Look at her. She's suffering, and we need to find help for her. Who will help us?"

"No one," said Nick. "But I know a way that we can help ourselves." He took a deep breath, searching her eyes. "There's a pawnshop on the wharves, further away than the one we usually use. It's got a loose latch on one of the windows. I noticed it yesterday when I was collecting wood; the owner was closing up the windows and couldn't get one of them to latch properly. It would be easy to open it and slip inside in the night."

Gwen swallowed hard. "Nick, you want us to break into a shop?"

"What choice do we have, Gwen?" said Nick. "There's plenty of valuables in there. We can steal them, sell them somewhere even if we have to go to another pawnshop further away to do it. Then we can get a doctor for Roberta."

Gwen stared down at her sister, listening to her ragged breathing. Roberta was in agony. Even though the very thought of breaking into someone's shop made Gwen's skin crawl, she knew that Nick was right: there was no other way. She had to save Roberta, no matter what it took from her.

If only she had never persuaded her mother to let Teddy go out begging. If only she had never decided to take them all to the workhouse. So many of her choices had been so wrong, and now she had to trust this one, too.

She looked up at Nick, her throat thick with tears. "All right," she said. "Let's do it."

~ ~ ~ ~ ~

The pawnshop looked unfamiliar in the insufficient light of the streetlamp on the corner. Even though Gwen had been there before – they had pawned stolen items all over their part of the city by this point – it still looked intimidating. The blinds were drawn over the one window that still had all of its glass; the other was boarded up. There was a hand-painted wooden sign over the door, stating simply, PAWNSHOP.

It wasn't the ground floor, however, that worried Gwen. It was the second story. She knew that the owner of the pawnshop must be sleeping up there, and if they woke him...

It was unthinkable. She pushed down her worries, forcing a smile for Roberta. "All right, Bobbie," she said, squeezing her sister's hand. "Are you sure you'll be all right to keep watch?"

"I'll be fine," said Roberta, her voice curt and sharp with pain.

"Sit here," said Nick, indicating a broken box lying near the street corner. "You'll have a good view of the streets, and you'll be able to see if the owner turns on a light upstairs."

"I'll shout if I see anything," said Roberta. She sat down slowly, wincing with pain, one hand rising involuntarily to her head.

"We'll soon have money for medicine and a doctor, Bobbie," said Gwen. "Just hold on a little bit longer. Soon you won't be in pain anymore."

"I know." Roberta gave her a weak, shaky smile.

It was that smile that gave Gwen the strength to turn and face the pawnshop. Nick rested a hand on her shoulder. "Let's get it done," he said.

They walked up to the front of the shop together, placing their feet quietly. Gwen's heart was hammering so loudly that she wondered at the fact it hadn't yet woken the owner. Nick crouched down by the lock, peering into it. One of the rough characters that he occasionally chatted with outside the warehouse had showed him how to pick a lock yesterday, but Gwen was still unsure if he'd get it right as he slid a piece of wire into the lock.

There were a few terse moments. Nick's face was lined with concentration; there was something powerful about the expression in the pale light, and even with fear and pain surrounding her, Gwen was struck for a moment by how wonderful he was. A pang of pain ran through her alongside the hopeless love. What good was the way she felt about him? Survival was nearly impossible; having any kind of a real life together someday, the kind of life they dreamed of, was nothing but a useless dream.

The lock clicked. Nick looked up at her, a grin splitting his face. She returned it almost without meaning to, and Nick slowly pushed the door open.

Blessedly, the hinges did not creak. The door opened a crack, and Gwen slipped through it first, quickly followed by Nick. He shut it soundlessly behind them, sealing them in musty, overcrowded darkness.

Gwen took a deep breath, knowing a moment of panic as the enclosed space reminded her terrifyingly of the refractory ward. Then Nick's hand found hers. "I'm here," he whispered.

She swallowed hard. "Let's hurry," she breathed.

Nick reached into his pocket and drew out a damp matchbox. Taking out one precious match, he struck it as quietly as he could against the wall, cupping a hand over it to reduce the light. Some light sneaked out between his fingers, catching a few objects in the glass cabinets behind the counter: a gold pocket watch, a collection of china vases, a medallion of some kind, and a pair of earrings that flashed like jewels.

"The watch, the medallion and the earrings," Nick hissed.

"I'll get the watch," Gwen whispered back.

She hurried towards it, her eyes trained on the flash of gold. She grasped the handle of the glass door and tugged; it wouldn't budge.

Glancing over at Nick, she saw that he already had his door open; he was reaching inside, taking hold of the medallion. The cabinets clearly weren't locked. Her body pounding with adrenalin, Gwen gripped the handle in both hands and yanked.

A terrible shudder ran through the entire cabinet, and it wobbled horribly towards her for a second before rocking back onto its feet with a dull thud. Gwen held her breath; Nick whipped around, staring at her, and every muscle in her body sprang tight with tension. But there was no sound from upstairs, nor any alarm from Roberta.

"Quick," whispered Nick, reaching inside again to grab the earrings.

Gwen tugged at the door again; it had come loose now, and swung open easily. Trembling all over with shock and fear, Gwen snatched the watch from the shelf.

It was only when the watch was already in her hands that she saw that one of the china vases had been leaning against it. It teetered; she lunged at it, but her fingers found only air, and the vase tumbled down to the ground. When it met the floor, it shattered with a deafening crash, tiny white pieces scattering across the floor like an explosion.

There was a great roaring sound from somewhere behind the pawnshop: the baying of dogs. Gwen looked up at Nick, frozen in terror.

"Light!" shouted Roberta's voice from outside. "Light!"

Nick grabbed Gwen's hand. "Run!" he shouted.

They bolted together, Gwen's feet slipping and sliding on the shattered china. Nick yanked the door open; as they rushed through it, there were footsteps on the stairs, and Gwen glanced back to see a figure in a dressing-gown crashing into the pawnshop. He was yelling incoherently, and it was only when they had already bolted into the street that Gwen realized what he was shouting.

"Get them!" he was yelling. "Sic them!"

"Run, Bobbie, run!" Nick screamed as they pounded down the street.

Roberta was stumbling to her feet. Gwen didn't dare to look back; she seized her sister's arm, and they ran, pell-mell, Roberta gasping with pain, Nick leading the way. Gwen expected him to lead them towards the warehouse, but at the end of the street he glanced back, and horror transfixed his face. Swinging hard to the right, he led them in the opposite direction – towards the wharves.

Clutching Roberta, Gwen followed him at full speed. She didn't want to know what it was that was chasing them that had frightened him so much, but she feared she already did.

The streets were very dark here, the smell of the Thames overpowering in every desperate gulp of air that Gwen drew into her lungs. Roberta stumbled beside her, weeping with pain, but there was no slowing down. They swung around another corner; Nick was looking up and down, left and right, seeking somewhere to go, but the shops and businesses were side-by-side here, with no handy alleyways or empty doorways to duck into.

Suddenly, a dead weight slammed down onto Gwen's arm. She stumbled, her shoulder wrenching; the paving met her knees with a devastating crack, and she screamed in pain. Roberta's arm had disappeared from her hand. Gwen looked back for her sister, and that was when she saw the dogs.

There were two of them, and they were enormous; two bundles of muscle wrapped in black skin, their paws flying silently over the paving as they charged towards Gwen, their white fangs flashing in the lamplight.

"Get up, Bobbie!" Gwen grabbed for her sister, who was making feeble attempts to rise – it seemed she had tripped on the curb. "Get up!"

Nick was suddenly beside her. He grabbed Roberta's arm and yanked her to her feet. "Keep going!" he shouted.

The dogs were nearly upon them. Gwen clung to Roberta and ran with all her failing strength; Nick was beside her, helping her, their feet slamming into the ground in arrhythmic chaos like a herd of frightened deer. They ducked around another corner; the dogs were still behind them, their barks at their very heels – and suddenly there was no more street ahead of them, just an expanse of black water, lights shimmering on its surface.

At once, the three of them stumbled to a halt, mere feet from the water's edge. They had reached the wharves. Ships loomed on their side of them, creaking quietly as they rocked against their moorings.

"Go. This way!" Nick gasped, yanking Gwen's hand to the left. He grabbed a pallet with his free hand, flinging it behind them as they ran; there was a yelp from the dogs, but only briefly before the baying continued. They were just a few yards behind. Gwen's heart thundered in her throat. She had never been so terrified.

"I can't. I can't!" Roberta cried, yanking hard on Gwen's arm. "I can't run," she gasped.

"You have to!" Gwen shouted.

But Roberta's head was lolling, her face ashen; her knees buckled as she ran, and she began to fall. Gwen gave a cry of dismay, scrambling to keep Roberta from falling. Nick grabbed the back of Roberta's dress, slowing her fall; Gwen tripped over her legs, and they both sank to the ground together.

"Bobbie!" Gwen gasped, wrapping her hands around Roberta's pale cheeks.

"Hide. Hide!" Nick yelled.

Gwen looked up, uncomprehending in her fear. There was a streetlamp behind them, and it illuminated the hard lines of determination on Nick's face. The dogs were bounding towards them, snarling. Nick glanced around, picked up a piece of broken plank that lay nearby, and stood waiting for them, holding the plank like a club.

"No! Nick!" Gwen screamed.

"Hide!" Nick shouted.

Roberta gave a moan of pain. Torn between them, Gwen grabbed Roberta's arms and dragged her towards the shadow of the nearest ship. They were almost there when the first of the dogs reached Nick.

It launched itself towards him, fangs flashing, claws outstretched; he swung the plank with all his might, catching the animal on the shoulder with enough impact to throw it to the ground. It spun across the paving, whimpering, and crashed into its companion. Both dogs fell and scrabbled on the paving. Both were already trying to get up.

Gwen had dragged Roberta into the shadow of the ship. She tucked herself, terrified, against a pile of barrels stacked in front of it; they were covered with a tarpaulin, and she grabbed one corner and pulled it over them both.

The dogs had risen. They approached Nick warily, hackles raised from head to tail, low snarls emitting from their jaws. He couldn't face them both at once. Backing away, he waved the plank at them, shouting breathlessly.

"Hey! Get back!" he gasped. "Go away!"

The bigger dog snapped at the plank. Nick lunged at it, and it jumped back a few steps, but never took its eyes off him. The other rushed in, snapping at Nick's leg; he cried out, and fabric ripped. The plank smacked against the dog's head, and it yelped, backing away.

"Nick!" Gwen cried, half rising to her feet.

"Stay there!" Nick shouted.

"Gwen?" Roberta stirred, lifting her head. "Ah! My head!"

"Shhh!" Gwen hissed, terrified.

The bigger dog was gathering itself for a leap. Gwen saw the muscles bunch in its haunches, and it jumped, lunging straight for Nick's face. He screamed in shock and swung the plank, smacking it into the dog's face; it snapped at the plank, seizing it in its jaws. Landing easily, the dog spun to face Nick, growling and shaking at the plank. His hands bare,

Nick backed away, but it was already too late. The other dog was rushing at him. It launched itself into the air, teeth bared for Nick's throat.

"No! Nick!" Gwen shrieked.

The dog struck Nick full in the chest, jaws snapping down towards flesh. He stumbled backwards and stepped out over the edge of the wharf. For a terrible moment, his feet scrabbled at the edge, but the weight of the dog was too much.

Nick fell without a sound, and vanished in a spray of water.

"Nick!" Gwen could hide no more. She rushed forth, her screams echoing across the wharves, towards the place where he had fallen. "NICK!"

There was blood in the water; it churned pink in the lamplight. Gwen rushed to the edge, falling to her knees, hands extended into it as though she could grasp him and pull him to safety. She couldn't swim. She wasn't sure if he could.

"Nick! No! Nick!" she screamed.

A low, rumbling sound on her right caught her attention. She looked up. The remaining dog was stalking towards her, its head low, yellow eyes blazing into hers.

The water had stopped churning. Gwen stood up, backing away, horribly conscious of Roberta lying under the tarpaulin several yards behind her. The dog's eyes were fixed on her now. What would happen if she jumped into the river seeking for Nick? Would it find Roberta?

She glanced into the water again. It had gone very still, and a terrible truth was taking hold of her heart, one too big for her to comprehend, one that would break her into a thousand pieces.

Nick was dead.

"G-Gwen?" Roberta's voice carried to her over the still night.

Tears gushed down Gwen's cheeks. Nick was gone, but she still had to save her sister — and to do that, she had to lead this dog away from Roberta's hiding place.

"Come on!" she yelled, clapping her hands. Startled, the dog jumped back, then kept snarling and stalking towards her. "Yes! That's right!" Gwen waved her arms. "Come and get me, you ugly brute!"

The dog snapped and lunged. Gwen spun on her heel, running for dear life into the maze of the wharves, the animal hot on her heels. Every stride took it further away from hurting her sister.

And every stride brought home the truth: there was nothing Gwen could do to save Nick.

~ ~ ~ ~ ~

Gwen ran until she could run no more, the dog hot on her heels with every step. She finally spotted a rope ladder hanging over the gunwale of a ship, and spent the last of her strength scrambling up it, where she clung to the top — too afraid to climb onto the deck — and listened to the dog barking and barking and barking below her. Its voice grew hoarse, and the minutes slid by with the rope cutting into her hands, but Gwen was hardly present here on the rough rope with the savage dog feet below her. She was back on the wharf, hearing Nick's last scream, seeing him tumble backwards into the water, seeing the water foam red with his blood.

She clung to the rope ladder and wept, not caring if she spent the rest of her life hanging here, or even if the dog climbed up somehow and killed her.

But it didn't. In fact, by the time Gwen's hands were rubbed raw from the rope and its own bark had grown hoarse, it finally turned around and slunk off into the shadows.

Gwen hung there for a few minutes longer, hardly daring to believe that the dog had gone, and almost paralyzed with grief and terror. She may have hung there forever if it hadn't been for the steady knowledge drumming through her mind that she had to get back to Roberta. Her sister was still lying under the tarpaulin, hurt and scared. Gwen at least had the gold watch in her pocket. She could still get Roberta some food and medicine...

She had gambled Nick's life to save Roberta's. Hot tears ran down her cheeks as she slowly, stiffly climbed down the ladder and fell to the ground, stumbling as she landed. What were they going to do without Nick?

He had always been her guiding light. But the world had grown cold and silent now, quieter and lonelier even than the refractory ward without him in it.

She blundered back in the direction she had run, barely able to move except for the constant urge that told her she had to get back to Roberta. Limping and staggering, blinded by tears, it was a long few moments until she reached the ship where she'd hidden her sister. She cast a hopeless glance down the length of the wharf, hoping that perhaps she would see Nick waiting there somehow. But of course, there was nothing. No dogs, no Nick... and no more hope in the world.

She turned away, looking into the shadows under the tarpaulin. "Bobbie?" she croaked out, her voice broken with tears.

There was no response. Gwen's heart flipped over. Had something happened to Roberta? She ran towards the tarpaulin. "Bobbie!" she shouted, grabbing the corner and throwing it back.

There was no one there.

Gwen stared down at the paving, panting, unable to comprehend what she was seeing. Was this the wrong place? But no, it was there beside the barrels, right where she had left her sister, and there was a bloodstain on the ground where Roberta had lain.

"Bobbie!" Gwen turned around, her eyes scanning the ships around her. She started to stumble from one shadow to the other, searching. "Bobbie! Bobbie!"

She searched until her cries grew weak and feeble, swallowed up by tears. There was no sign of Roberta.

There was no sign of anyone that Gwen had loved. She had lost them all.

Part Four

Chapter Ten

Three Years Later

Gwen plunged the scrubbing brush back into the bucket of water. It had been barely lukewarm when she had drawn it in the first place; Mr. Pennington didn't have any means of heating it other than placing a pot on the fire, and coal was precious here. Now, many hours into her work, the water was ice cold and soupy with dirt.

She tried to ignore the cold that stung her chapped fingers and the broken edges of the brush that pressed splinters into her skin, turning her focus instead to the last section of flooring that needed to be scrubbed out. Working the brush across the stone, she tried her best, as she had been doing all day, to lose herself in the simple rhythm of the work: the hiss of the bristles on the floor, the cramps building slowly in her arms, the pain in her knees from constant pressure.

It was easier to lose herself in these small agonies than to let her mind wander, and sink into the quagmire of sorrow in her heart.

When she finished the last corner of the room and sat back on her heels, the sun was sinking, and the last traces of evening light had filled the room with gold. Gwen glanced over the clean floor, allowing her heart a moment's satisfaction in a job well done.

"Are you finished already, Gwendoline?" spoke a kindly old voice from the doorway.

Gwen got up stiffly, her legs trembling with the effort, and tossed the brush back into the bucket. "Yes, Mr. Pennington," she said, lifting the bucket and turning to face him. "If it's to your satisfaction, sir."

"Your work always is, dear," said Mr. Pennington. He was a bent little old man, his skin blotched and spotted with wear and his hands twisted from work, but there was still a fresh kindness in his green eyes that Gwen seldom saw anywhere else. "I have to say, I thought it was just charity when the missus asked you to wash our floors twice a week, but I wish I could pay you more. You do such good work."

"The workhouse trained me well, sir," said Gwen, dredging up a smile. She knew full well that Mrs. Pennington had only offered her the twice-weekly job out of compassion; two years ago, Gwen had been wild-eyed and starving after her first winter on the streets alone. She would have died were it not for the kindness of these two old people.

As it was, her body ached with hunger. The heel of bread that Mrs. Pennington had given her for lunch had been her first meal in three days.

"Here you are then," said Mr. Pennington, reaching into his pocket for a few pennies. "I would give you more if I could, Gwendoline." He paused. "Do you still have somewhere safe to sleep?"

Gwen longed to tell him the truth, to say that she didn't. Perhaps he'd give her a corner of his shop to sleep in. But she knew that his landlord frowned upon Gwen's very presence there, even if she was working. She didn't want to get the sweet Penningtons into trouble.

"Yes, sir," she lied. "Thank you."

Taking the money, she left the cobbler's shop behind and walked out into a frigid evening. The light that had been so warm when it came into the shop was useless now in the face of the sharp-toothed wind that howled around the corners and snatched at Gwen's threadbare clothes. It stole her breath, and she stopped after a few steps, trembling with exhaustion, knowing that the pennies in her hand would feed her for a day or two, and after that hunger was inevitable.

She felt as though she was groping in total darkness, searching desperately for the light. But the light in her life had been snuffed out that night on the wharves. Every day, it was getting harder to keep on trying.

But she had one reason left to live. Gritting her teeth against the pain, Gwen moved on.

~ ~ ~ ~ ~

For the first year after Nick died and Roberta disappeared, Gwen had stayed around their old neighbourhood, searching up and down for her sister despite the fact that painful memories were around every corner. It was only once she had given up on finding Roberta near the wharves that she finally permitted herself to leave the wharves behind and move deeper into London.

Like so much of the exhausted debris of humanity that lived in this squalid city, Gwen had been washed up on the shores of the Old Nichol. The streets had grown more familiar to her now, and she followed them mindlessly, twisting and turning between tenement buildings with holey walls and long stretches where nothing was taller than her head; every building was more of a shelter, cobbled together with driftwood and rags. Listless eyes watched her as she passed. She didn't look up at them; instead, she kept her eyes trained on the dirt, trying her best to avoid the more noxious puddles and the decaying bodies of rats and frogs that lay everywhere.

Finally, pushing into a cloud of putrid smoke, Gwen walked into the marketplace that served the poorest of London's poor. There were no shelters over these stalls; instead, people plied their trade on planks balancing on broken barrels, or on stacks of old wooden boxes. A stench of rotten fish hung over everything.

Gwen knew she should just get some bread from the man who sold loaves that were only a little mouldy, but her stomach growled at the sight of the old woman with the gruel. She hadn't eaten anything hot in so long. Her feet carried her over to where the woman sat, bent almost double, on an old box and stirred the cast-iron pot with a stick. It bubbled thickly on its little fire of damp coal.

"A bowl, please," said Gwen, holding out ha'penny.

The old woman looked up at her through strings of grimy hair. She took the penny, secreting it somewhere in the dusty folds of her garments, then produced a cracked wooden bowl. Giving a wet and noisy sniff, she dragged one hand over her nose, then reached for a wooden spoon lying on the ground and scooped some of the gruel into the bowl.

Gwen almost snatched it from the old woman's hands. Heedless of how grubby her own hands were, she plunged her fingers into the scalding gruel and gulped it down in greedy mouthfuls that burned her tongue and throat. She didn't care about the heat; the feeling of having something warm sliding into her stomach was intoxicating. Even though the food was all but tasteless, she could feel some strength returning to her body.

Licking out the very last scraps, Gwen looked over the top of the bowl, glancing around the marketplace almost out of habit. Now that she had eaten something, she had the strength to continue doing the one thing that still kept her going: searching. Her eyes locked on the face of every person that passed her, searching for a pair of soft blue eyes. Even though it had been three years since the last time Gwen had seen Roberta, she would never forget the exact hue of her sister's eyes.

Wandering away from the old woman with the gruel, Gwen began to move through the crowds as she always did, looking at every face, peering under every shadowy hood even when people flinched back and cursed at her. She didn't care what anyone did to her.

Finding Roberta was the last hope she had left.

~ ~ ~ ~ ~

It was only when the crowds had completely thinned out, and the spark of hope had grown very low in Gwen's heart, that she came to the same painful realization as she did every night: that today was not the day in which she would find her sister.

She had not lasted long in the warehouse alone. Nick had fought off gangs of homeless children several times in the year that he had lived there with Gwen and Roberta; without him, Gwen was powerless to defend her home. That warehouse was miles away now as she stumbled, exhausted, along yet another empty street. Her eyes ached from the effort of straining to see every face she passed. Even her voice was tired from shouting her sister's name in the vain hope that somewhere out there, Roberta would hear, and finally run into Gwen's arms again.

But not today. Gwen tried not to think about how many days like this one had passed, days of desperate searching. Her eyes rested on the doorway of a shop; there didn't seem to be anyone close by, and at least it was out of the wind. She walked over to it and sank down on the cold, hard doorstep, trying to get her shoulders comfortable against the door.

She would search again tomorrow. At least she had some money left for bread; she could walk further if she had eaten, continuing to widen the radius around Mr. Pennington's shop as she searched every crowd and street she could for her sister. Maybe tomorrow would be the day that she finally found her.

She told herself this, wrapping her arms around her cold body against the shivers that scampered up and down her spine. She told herself that she would find Roberta, the way she had been telling herself for years. That her sister was out there somewhere, alive and well, and searching for Gwen just as Gwen was searching for her.

She told herself that Roberta had not died that night, that she hadn't gotten up in her disoriented state and stumbled into the wharves, and drowned, and sunk to the bottom of the Thames just like Nick...

Tears coursed down Gwen's face. Her body was too exhausted to sob; the wind cooled the tears on her cheeks, and she silently cried herself to sleep.

~ ~ ~ ~ ~

The next morning, Gwen could no longer stand the loneliness of the streets.

She sat on the doorstep at dawn, watching the sky turn grey with the growing light, and stared into the bustle of people heading off to work. At any moment, one of them would turn aside to unlock the door where Gwen was sitting. They would kick her, probably, and call her names. She should get up and move and keep searching for Roberta.

Yet today, her heart was failing her. She wasn't sure she could survive one more day of stumbling through the city, alone and hungry, searching for a sister who might not even be alive anymore. If she hadn't yet found Roberta in three years of searching, was it even possible to find her at all?

Gwen's eyes were resting habitually on the faces of every stranger that past her. In the grey light, they all seemed as hard and unyielding as stone. No one bothered to glance aside at the thin figure huddled on the doorstep. No one cared if she lived or died.

Gwen herself no longer cared.

The realization drove her to her feet with a ripple of cold fear. Had her life come to this, that it was worth nothing anymore, even to her?

She shivered on the sidewalk, arms wrapped around her bony body. She couldn't go on like this. She had to talk to someone who cared about her, someone who was more than just the Pennington's – someone who was family.

If she couldn't find Roberta, she would have to find someone else. She would have to go back to Mama.

Tears rushed down her cheeks at the memory of her mother, sickly and abused, the last time she had seen her. That had been only a few months ago; Gwen had made a habit of visiting her mother at the workhouse yard from time to time, always keeping watch for Mrs. Webb to make sure she didn't get her mother into trouble. Mama always asked about Roberta. Gwen had lied every time, telling her mother that Roberta was just fine.

She would have visited Mama every day if she could, instead of once every few months.

But shame had always stopped her: shame that she had lost Roberta, just like she'd lost Joey and Teddy. But now even her shame was not larger than her loneliness.

Gwen took a deep, shaky breath and turned to her left. She could reach the workhouse in a day, and be back here in time to scrub Mr. Pennington's floors the day after tomorrow. Perhaps Mama would be dead this time. Perhaps Mama would find out the truth somehow, and hate her, the way she had hated her when Teddy died.

But at least visiting Mama gave her something to live for, just for this day, just for this hour.

~ ~ ~ ~ ~

Even four years later, the sight of the workhouse's stern lines and sharp corners still sent chills down

Gwen's spine as she walked up the street towards it. She had to stop a few yards from the corner of the nearest courtyard; the memories that struck her were just too painful to endure. Previously, she had always hated seeing the workhouse because it reminded her of Mrs. Webb's rage.

Now, she couldn't bear seeing the workhouse because it reminded her of Nick's love.

She closed her eyes, allowing tears to slide down her cheeks. The memory that lanced through her was as exquisitely painful as a hot poker to the chest. Sneaking through the dark hallways to see Roberta. Thanking Nick for the risk he was taking by helping her. *You're worth it*, he had said, his brown eyes deep and warm.

She wasn't worth it. She hadn't been worth it: Nick had been thrown onto the streets for helping her, and it had gotten him killed.

Joey, Teddy, Nick, maybe even Roberta... would there ever be an end to the people Gwen loved who died because of her?

It was by a sheer force of will, toiling against the incomprehensible weight of her own guilt, that Gwen made her way to the corner of the courtyard where Mama normally sat picking oakum. She pressed her forehead against the bars, tears splashing on the paving at her feet, and looked into the ranks of women. There were many of them, sitting in rows, their hands gnarled with work, their skin bruised and weathered, all in their faded dresses with the workhouse stripes. Gwen's eyes moved automatically from one face to the next. Searching for familiarity had become automatic for her.

But she didn't find it here.

Her heart thumped painfully. Gwen searched again. She must have missed Mama... she had to be here. But she was sure this time: Mama wasn't here in this courtyard.

Gwen looked up towards the front door of the workhouse, her heart thumping painfully in her chest. She had to know what happened to Mama – even if it meant facing Mrs. Webb again. Mama could be the last family she had left.

No. Don't think that. Bobbie is out there somewhere. The words she had repeated to herself so many times fell flat now.

Gwen limped slowly up the street to the front gate of the workhouse with its spikes and bars. When she looked through it, a part of her still expected to see a young Nick waiting there for her with his free smile and his gentle words. *Good morning! How can I help you?* She had heard him speak those words to so many desperate souls as she mopped the hallway.

But the young man leaning against the gate was nothing like Nick. He was thin and scruffy, with watery eyes that glanced her over with disdain.

"What do you want?" he said. "We're full. You can't come in."

Gwen knew that Mrs. Webb would never have let her in anyway. She approached the gate timorously, summoning the last scraps of her courage.

"Please, sir," she said. "I just want to ask about someone in the workhouse."

"We don't allow visitors," said the porter.

"I know that," said Gwen quickly. "Oh, I know you're very busy, sir. I would never have the audacity to request a visit. I just want to know if this person is still in the workhouse."

The boy regarded her for a few moments with a mixture of boredom and suspicion. Leaning against the gate, he folded his arms.

"Please, sir, I don't want to waste your time," said Gwen, hoping that flattery would work in him where common sympathy appeared to be absent. "I know you have important things to do."

"Very well, then." The porter sniffed. "Tell me the name of this person of yours, and I'll see if I can remember it."

Gwen swallowed hard. She knew that this was the only chance she would get to inquire about her mother, and she could only hope that the porter knew her name. Mama had been in the workhouse for many years, after all; perhaps he would know her. It was far too much to hope that he would be bothered to find it out if he didn't know.

"It's Hopewell, sir," she said. "Bertha Hopewell. She's my mother." Her voice cracked a little on the last syllable, and she swallowed hard to control her tears.

"Hopewell, Hopewell," muttered the porter. "Oh – I do know her. At least, I did." He shrugged, tucking his hands into his pockets. "She's not here."

"Not here?" Gwen's heart thudded painfully against her ribs. "What do you mean, she's not here?"

"Exactly what I said. She's gone." The porter straightened, irritation flashing in his eyes. "You're wasting my time."

"Sir, please!" Gwen cried, leaping forward and grabbing the porter's arm. "Please, just tell me what happened. Tell me where she is!"

The porter's lip curled in an angry snarl. He gave her a brutal shove, knocking her backwards; her weak limbs failed her, and she fell heavily to the ground, jarring pain running up her arm where she had thrown it out to break her fall.

"Get out of my sight, you filthy little wench," he spat.

"Sir, please!" Gwen cried.

But it was no use. The porter had turned his back and was striding swiftly back towards the workhouse, and Gwen could do nothing except dissolve in a pool of tears.

She should never have come here. Now, she didn't know whether Mama lived or died, any more than she knew Roberta's fate.

Chapter Eleven

The only place where Mama could have survived was in another workhouse.

Gwen had been to three other workhouses in the two weeks since she had learned that Mama was no longer in the workhouse where she and Roberta had lived. The porters there had all received her with varying shades of anger and disdain; her efforts to get information from them, and to peer over the walls into the courtyards were the women worked, had earned her nothing but bruises and the knowledge that Mama wasn't there. She had asked after Roberta, too. She didn't think Roberta would ever have gone back into a workhouse of her own accord, but she had to try.

She had to try. She kept telling herself that she had to try as she limped up another long street, heading towards the workhouse at the far side of Whitechapel. It was a long way from the streets of the Old Nichol where she worked for Mr. Pennington, but Gwen had searched all the other workhouses near her. She hoped she would be able to make her way back to Mr. Pennington's shop in time to do her work tomorrow morning. It had been two days since she had spent her last penny on a chunk of stale bread and a wrinkled apple.

The apple had been floury and sour, but the memory of it still made Gwen's mouth water. She sank down on a street corner, exhausted. She knew that the workhouse was somewhere around here, perhaps one block away, perhaps four or five, but she couldn't take one more step without a brief rest.

A smell accosted her, and Gwen looked up. This was a back street, and rows of garbage cans were standing here being what smelled like butcheries and bakeries. Fermenting garbage waited to be taken away. The can nearest Gwen had something that looked like bread sticking out of the top.

Gwen struggled to her feet and picked up the piece of bread. It was soggy and wet; when she raised it to her lips, the sour smell turned her stomach, and she tossed it back into the can. But she thought she could glimpse something else further down – it looked like a potato. If it was only a little green, she could eat it. It wouldn't be her first raw potato.

Gwen stood on tiptoe to lean into the can, pushing aside the heaps of fermenting food and broken glass. She stretched down, her fingertips just brushing the surface of the potato, and that was when a voice rang out from somewhere in front of her.

"Oi! You!"

Nothing good ever came of those two words. Gwen flinched back, the tantalizing hope of food slipping between her fingers, and looked up into an angry face. A man was standing at the back door of his shop, his butcher's apron smeared with animal blood.

"What are you doing?" he barked.

"Sir, I'm just – I'm just hungry," Gwen whimpered. She started to back away, knowing that trouble was coming.

An iron hand descended on the back of her dress, gripping the fabric hard. Gwen squealed and jumped, twisting to see the man who had captured her; he had a face as hard and puckered as weathered stone.

"Got her, guv," he said. "What do you want me to do with her?"

The butcher shook his head. "Teach her a lesson," he snapped, turning around. "We can't have her type hanging about and stealing from our bins."

Gwen's blood turned to ice. She stared up into the face of her captor, and saw something ugly in his eyes as they roved over her emaciated body.

"And make it quick, Larry," the butcher called over his shoulder. "We have customers to serve."

"Sure, guv," Larry called.

The door slammed, and Gwen was left alone with Larry in this cold street, and he was looking at her hungrily. "Let me go!" she shrieked, throwing herself against his grip. "Let me go! Help! Somebody help!"

"No, no," spat Larry, smacking a hard hand down over Gwen's mouth. Her screams grew horribly muffled. "You did this to yourself," he hissed, switching the hand on her dress to grip her hair with ripping pain. Dragging her by her hair and face, he forced her up against the back wall of the butchery, pressing his body against hers.

Gwen knew absolute panic. She was trapped, and she knew exactly what he was going to do to her, and no one would hear her screams. Fear lent strength to her tired limbs, and somehow she twisted around, hair ripping from her head, to claw blindly at his face with both hands. His hands found her throat; her screams were strangled, and he slammed her back against the wall with an impact that sent blackness bursting through her vision. Dazed and desperate, Gwen scrabbled at his hands, but they might as well have been iron shackles around her throat.

There was no way out. She lashed out blindly with her limbs, and her knee hit something that yielded.

Larry let out a bellow of rage. His hands disappeared from her throat, and Gwen fell to her hands and knees, choking and gasping, saliva dripping from her open mouth as she gasped for air.

Larry was bellowing, bent double; she found her way to her feet, clawing at her throat, and bolted before he could recover.

She couldn't run far. Every breath burned her throat; her strength had been all but spent in the struggle. She made it around the corner and up the next block before she scrambled down the next street to her left and collapsed in an empty doorway, clutching her throat and retching up gobs of saliva and blood.

It seemed that Larry had not pursued her. Gwen leaned against the doorway, shivering uncontrollably until her breathing became more normal. There was a terrible stinging pain in the back of her head. She reached up to touch it, and her fingers found something sticky. When she lowered her hand, it was smeared with blood.

Gwen stared down at the redness on her fingers, knowing exactly what it meant.

She was hurt. Her mind felt sluggish; when she looked up at the street, her vision blurred, objects swimming in and out of focus. It took her a few moments to work out whether there was one lamppost in front of her, or two.

Tears rushed quietly down her cheeks. She was alone and hurt and hungry. There was no way she could make it back to the Pennington's, not in this state. How would she survive?

She stared up the street as if for inspiration, and her eyes found a tall building with sharp lines and bare brick walls. The sign above the door took her a few moments to read, her eyes finding the letters one by one... *Workhouse*.

Everything inside her despaired at the sight of it. She had been fighting to escape this fate, this imprisonment far away from where she could search for Roberta, for so many years.

Yet still it had found her. It was dragging her to her inevitable and miserable destiny, and she was powerless against it.

Gwen stumbled to her feet and started walking. One foot after the other, she approached the workhouse door, and as she went, she felt herself giving up. Giving up on finding Roberta. Giving up on finding Mama. She had clung to the hope of finding Roberta again for so, so long, but it was time to accept that she was gone, just like Joey and Teddy. It was time to accept that she lost everything she loved, that no good thing could stay in her life. Sooner or later, she would ruin everything. She would destroy everything that was good.

As the workhouse door was closer, she felt a strange sense of relief. It was easier to give up hope. It took away the wrenching sadness, and left her only with a sense of steady regret: regret that she had been born into her family, and forced herself with all of her bad luck on the people she loved.

A thought struck her, stopping her in her tracks.

She hadn't forced herself on Nick.

She thought of the night she had hidden under a bench in the dining hall of the workhouse, when Mrs. Webb had searched for her, and Nick had told her that there was no one there – even though he knew full well that Gwen was hiding there. He had chosen to stick out his neck for her, no matter what it would cost him.

Nick had chosen her.

The memory sent tears sliding down her cheeks. Nick had chosen to help her, again and again. He had chosen to keep taking her to see Roberta. He had chosen to stand up for her and get himself thrown on the street with her and Roberta. He had chosen to stay with them.

And ultimately, he had chosen to give his life to save her and her sister.

You're worth it. His words echoed in her soul, and suddenly it didn't matter that she didn't believe them. Nick had believed them: that was enough.

Gwen looked up at the workhouse and squared her shoulders. She turned away and started to limp down the street, one step at a time.

She was going to find Roberta. No matter what it took.

~ ~ ~ ~ ~

Gwen never did make it back to the Pennington's.

She was thinking about them now as she sat on the corner of a crowded market square. This place lacked the smokiness and sour smells of the marketplace she'd known in the Old Nichol.

Instead, the people here were clean and well-dressed; they laughed and chattered as they made their way among the shops instead of moping around ramshackle stalls. Most of them were women, carrying baskets on their arms and wearing ribbons in their hair, some dressed in starched black-and-white uniforms.

The shopkeepers behind the glass windows of these shops all had rosy cheeks and bright smiles. They looked much more handsome and prosperous than Mr. Pennington. Still, Gwen saw the sidelong glances they gave her where she sat on the sidewalk in a ragged and filthy heap. Their nice smiles all hid hearts far uglier than that of wrinkly old Mr. Pennington.

She missed him and Mrs. Pennington, but she hadn't been able to go back. She had been surprised even to wake the day after she was attacked, sleeping under some old newspapers in an alley.

Moving had been almost impossible; she had dragged herself from one street corner to the other, seeking a place to beg.

If she hadn't found this place, she would have died weeks ago. The pickings were good here. Most of the people were rich enough to spare a few pennies but not so rich that they knew nothing of hardship, and there was a messy little courtyard behind the millinery that no one ever swept out. She had been sleeping there in comparative peace ever since; the milliner had spotted her a time or two, but always pretended not to notice. Even now that she might survive the journey back to the Old Nichol, Gwen had decided to stay. She'd searched that old and filthy slum for Roberta and found nothing.

Perhaps she would find her here, in the back streets around this marketplace, or working as a maid for one of these prosperous ladies.

A housekeeper bustled past her, just a few feet away. She was a handsome woman, stern in her uniform, and carried a rolled-up shopping list like a weapon. Gwen struggled to her knees, ignoring the aches in her back from sleeping on the ground.

"Excuse me, ma'am, if you please," she said.

The housekeeper stopped, her eyes glancing briefly over Gwen. For a moment, Gwen thought she would simply move on as so many people did, but instead she gave a deep sigh and started to dig in her purse.

"Thank you, ma'am," said Gwen, "but there's something I want more than money."

The housekeeper raised a bored eyebrow. "What could you need more than money?" she asked.

"The answer to a simple question." Gwen took a deep breath. "Do you know Roberta Hopewell? She's my sister, and I'm looking for her."

The housekeeper flicked a penny into the air. Gwen held out both hands and just managed to catch it.

"I don't," she said. "Godspeed to you."

Turning, she strode off, and Gwen looked down at the shiny penny in her hands. It wasn't as good as information about Roberta, but at least it was something.

She rose to her feet stiffly and began to move towards the bakery. If she went around to the back entrance and asked nicely, the baker would occasionally give her a heel of bread for a penny, and her stomach was growling despite the richer pickings she'd found here.

The baker was in a good mood after all, and the crust that he pressed into Gwen's hands in exchange for the penny was still fresh and warm. As she walked back out onto the sidewalk, Gwen pressed the bread to her lips and inhaled its fragrance deeply, her mouth-watering at its freshness. She stood on the sidewalk and began to tear into it in hungry bites, trying her best to slow down and chew so that the bread would last longer, yet desperate to bring something into her aching stomach.

She was gazing into the street, not concentrating, when a girl of surpassing beauty walked by.

Gwen barely caught a glimpse of her at all. She just saw her profile for a second as she walked past; then she was moving on, her back to Gwen, turning to listen to the young lady who was accompanying her. Still, that glance alone was enough to make Gwen freeze and stare after her. There had been round cheeks with a robust bloom; a curly lock of red-gold hair; perhaps even a glimpse of bright blue eyes...

Indescribably blue eyes. From behind, as she began to disappear into the crowd, the girl looked too tall and slim and grown up to be Roberta. But those eyes...

Gwen almost dropped the piece of bread. Thrusting it into her pocket instead, she ran out onto the street, heedless of the crush of people around her.

"Bobbie!" she shouted. "Bobbie!"

There were people everywhere. Gwen could only see the back of a pretty straw hat receding rapidly into the crowd. She shoved past a few people, eliciting gasps from shocked strangers, and raised her voice.

"Bobbie, wait!" she shouted. "It's me, Gwen. It's me! It's me!"

But there were people talking everywhere, and the straw hat didn't turn around. Gwen pushed through the crowd, panting, desperate. "Bobbie!" she shouted. "Bobbie!"

It was no use. The straw hat vanished into the crush of people, and Gwen lost her for a few dry-mouthed moments. She pushed on, ignoring the yelps of surprise and indignation all around her. She just had to find Roberta...

She shoved her way to the edge of the crowd and found herself at the end of the street, where the shops ended and the road began. Looking around wildly, Gwen thought she had lost her.

Then, a cab came rattling past, the cabbie calling, "Whoa!" as he pulled on the reins. Gwen turned as it came to a halt off to her right, and saw the girl with the straw hat stepping up into the cab.

"Bobbie!" Gwen shouted.

She was too far away. The cab door slammed behind her, and the cab began to move off. Gwen jogged after it for a few steps before realizing her foolishness.

That couldn't be Roberta. Not looking so healthy, not dressed so well... Roberta would be thin and ragged, just like Gwen.

Then the girl looked back over her shoulder, and for a moment, her eyes met Gwen's through the glass of the back window.

They were blue after all. An indescribable blue. A colour Gwen had never seen before.

The cab turned the corner and disappeared, and Gwen knew that she had just seen her sister.

It felt as though her heart was swelling, as though it would explode in her chest. Tears coursed down her cheeks, tears of both joy and agony.

Roberta was alive. But she hadn't turned around when Gwen called her name.

THE WAIF'S LOST FAMILY

Chapter Twelve

The sky above Gwen's head felt heavy and miserable with coming winter.

It was only November, but Gwen's fingers ached with cold where she crouched on the street corner. She nearly forgot to raise her tin cup and say, "Alms for the poor?" when people pushed past. Her eyes were too busy searching through the crowd, looking eagerly for a pretty girl in a straw hat, for Roberta.

It had been two weeks since Gwen had seen Roberta in this market square.

She was more sure than ever that she really had seen her sister, and even though her heart ached with confusion over why Roberta hadn't heeded Gwen's cries, it didn't stop her from longing to see her again. She would run up to her and grab her hands and force her to look at her if she had to.

At least now she knew that Roberta was alive.

The thought was carrying her through the trials of coming winter. The cold, dry wind that howled around the market square every day tugged at Gwen's clothing and pierced her insufficient dress, slicing easily through the threadbare cloth. She shivered from morning until night, and it only made her hunger worse.

She knew that the only reason why she was still alive at all was because of the courtyard behind the millinery that she slept in at night. There was an overhang right up against the wall where she could sleep out of the wind and rain, and it wouldn't be long before she'd have to give up on begging and get back to her shelter. To be soaked by rain now would be death, as certainly as it had been for Teddy all those years ago.

Gwen shook her head sharply, as if to dislodge the memory. She gave her tin cup another rattle, hoping to draw the attention of one of the muffled passers-by in their hats and coats and scarves. "Alms?" she said through chattering teeth. "Alms?"

A slim figure paused nearby, her face covered by her scarf. She leaned down and Gwen looked eagerly up into her eyes, her heart leaping with hope for a moment. But as kind as those eyes were, they were green, not blue. A white hand was drawn from the depths of the coat, and a few coins rattled in the bottom of Gwen's cup.

"Thank you kindly, ma'am, thank you," breathed Gwen, trying to hide her disappointment.

The eyes smiled for a moment, and the young lady hurried off to a warm house with a fire and a family.

Gwen sank back to the ground, remembering the fantasies that Nick had always constructed for her, fantasies of a home with enough food and love to go around. Nick was gone, and so was that dream – but if she could only find Roberta, at least life would be bearable.

Hunger was clawing at her belly. She got up stiffly, her chapped hands aching with cold where she wrapped them around the mug with its precious few coins, and hurried over to the grocery. The pennies were enough to buy two wilted carrots and a knobby potato; she ate the potato first, biting into its cold and crunchy flesh, because hunger made it impossible to taste its starchy rawness.

Gnawing on the end of one of the carrots, Gwen headed towards her courtyard. There was a loud *splot* beside her; she looked down to see a dark circle of moisture on the pavement. Looking up into the grey sky, Gwen received the next raindrop on her cheek; the impact was surprisingly hard and cold, and it ran down her face like a tear.

It wouldn't be long before the heavens opened into a true deluge. Gwen pulled her coat a little tighter around her shoulders and ran for the courtyard as more raindrops started to fall around her, huge and slow and fat. Soon they would be pelting.

She scrambled onto a wobbly barrel, grasped the top of the wall, pulled herself over it, and dropped down into the messy little courtyard. Her nook was in the back corner; she headed straight for it, ready to wrap herself in some discarded bits of fabric and wait out the storm in the comparative warmth.

"Oi! What are you doing in here?"

Gwen froze. Turning slowly, she faced the back door of the millinery.

As she moved, her brain registered details that had escaped her in her hurry: the lack of mess, the garbage cans that had all been lined up neatly against one wall.

A young man was standing in the back door, arms akimbo. His face was sharp, eyes cold above the waxed ends of his moustache.

"Who are you?" he demanded.

"I – I'm Gwen," Gwen stammered out. "I sleep here."

"In the courtyard?" The man's eyes hardened. "You're a trespasser."

"No, sir, no," said Gwen.

"Oh? So Mrs. Gregory let you sleep in here, did she?"

Gwen swallowed hard. "Yes, sir," she said, hoping that this was the case.

The man folded his arms. "Well, I won't," he said. "My mother is much too soft – and sloppy. Look at the mess back here!" He gestured angrily. "I'm glad her illness forced her to ask me for help. Everything is a mess. And you're part of the mess."

"Sir, please." Gwen heard the drumming of the rain on the millinery roof, felt the drops slapping on top of her head. "It's raining. Please... let me have one more night here. I'll be gone in the morning. It's so cold."

"You're trespassing on my property," snapped the man, turning away. "If you don't leave now, I'll call the police."

Police. The word sent a thrill of cold fear through Gwen. She backed away, knowing that imprisonment would be the end of searching for Roberta.

"Sir..." she began.

The man glanced over his shoulder with a dismissive wave of his hand. "Go on, now," he said. "Or you'll regret it."

The finality in his tone made it clear that he was serious. Gwen turned and clambered onto one of the garbage cans, scrambling back over the wall. She landed heavily on the other side, nearly slipping on the wet pavement.

Shivering, she wrapped her arms around herself and gazed at the market square. The streets were emptying rapidly, people jumping into cabs, hurrying off out of the cold.

But she had nowhere to go.

Suddenly, the heavens truly opened. Rain started to come down in sheets; buffeting wind drove it against Gwen's body, enveloping her in indescribable cold. In a matter of seconds, she was wet through.

She ran to the only shelter she could see: a foot's overhang on the corner of the street. Huddling against the shop wall, Gwen tried her best to tuck her body under the overhang, but it was impossible. The driving wind just keep slamming rain against her face, against her trembling body.

She curled herself into a ball, covering her face with her arms. The wind went on howling. The rain kept on coming.

~ ~ ~ ~ ~

Gwen knew she was delirious.

Everything seemed to swim in front of her eyes as she sat on her corner, propped up against a lamppost, her breaths coming in rattling gasps. Every gasp set fire to her throat and chest; her lungs were toiling, and her back, ribs, and shoulders hurt with the sheer effort of breathing.

The fever had started two or three days after that storm. The rain had stopped somewhere in the middle of the night; Gwen's clothes had only dried out somewhere in the afternoon of the next day, in a bitterly cold wind. She had not been surprised when she had woken up one morning to find that her perpetual hunger had gone, replaced by a shakiness and nausea, her tongue so dry that it stuck to the roof of her mouth.

The cough had followed shortly after that. Now she doubted she had the strength to cough at all, even though she could feel the phlegm in her lungs with each laboured breath. She could tell by the way that everyone else on the square was dressed that it must be bitterly cold, yet she had untied the piece of strength that held her coat closed. She felt so warm. Everything she touched seemed icy.

She knew she should be trying to get some money, trying to find an apothecary that would help her, trying to find food. But in her heart, she knew that none of it would do any good. She had seen all this before in Teddy. She knew how this story would end.

If it was going to end, however, she was going to spend her last moments doing the one thing that had ever given her life meaning: she was going to look for Roberta. She was going to do everything she could for what family she had left.

It was difficult at times to focus on the faces of the people passing her. Her eyes felt tired; her vision blurred from time to time, her head swimming. She had to take rest breaks every now and then, closing her eyes and leaning her head back against the lamppost. Perhaps she slept a little from time to time. It was hard to tell.

She must have slept for a while later that afternoon, for when she opened her eyes, the streets were growing quiet. Dusk was settling in calm shades of twilit purple on the streets; the lamplighter was going from one post to the other, bringing golden circles of light to the streets. There were only a few people on the sidewalk now, hurrying home with brown paper parcels cuddled in their arms.

One of them was Nick.

Gwen knew she was hallucinating. Nick was dead, after all, and even when he was alive he had never looked like this. He was wearing a well-cut coat that hung down to his knees and made him look taller than ever; over the turned-up collar, his cheekbones looked perfectly chiselled. The honey-gold thatch of his hair was sticking out from under a warm, woolly hat with a grey pom-pom at the top. He was coming out of the bakery with a brown paper back in his gloved hands, the golden light from inside warming the smooth tones of his skin, lighting up the darkness of his brown eyes.

Even though it was only a fantasy, Gwen couldn't take her eyes off him. Perhaps her mind was trying to comfort her in her final moments, showing her this breath-taking vision of what could have been. This was all just a fever dream, yet she couldn't look away.

He stood at the doorway of the bakery, looking around, his brown eyes focused. He seemed to be searching for something. Somehow, Gwen knew that it was her that he was looking for.

She rose to her feet. It was a dream, after all; her body here wasn't constrained by illness. Still, she felt pangs of pain and weakness through her body as she shuffled off the sidewalk, uncaring about the traffic on the street, and dragged herself a few steps towards him.

"Nick?" She had meant to shout his name, but it came out as a croak.

He turned to face her. The wind ruffled his hair, pushing it over his eyes, but they still widened in recognition. She was struggling to hear now; the world was swimming, darkening at the edges, but she saw his lips form her name.

Maybe this was no dream. Maybe she was already dead, and he was welcoming her to Heaven.

She wanted to go to him. She wanted to leave the pain behind and fall into his arms, and she struggled for another step, but her limbs wouldn't respond. She felt herself falling and braced herself for the cold paving – and felt arms instead, strong arms folding around her, lowering her into a warm lap.

"Gwen." She heard his voice then, faintly, as though from a great distance.

She looked up. His eyes were so beautiful, even more beautiful than loving memory could preserve. He was holding her in his lap; his eyes were full of tears, and one of them slid down his cheek.

"No. Don't cry," she whispered. "Don't cry." She wanted so much for him to be as happy as she was, here with him, wherever they were.

She raised a grubby hand to his clean cheek and touched her fingertips to it, stopping the tears from running. The movement spent the last of her strength. Darkness overwhelmed her.

~ ~ ~ ~ ~

Something was stroking Gwen's hair.

Through the haze of overwhelming pain that flooded her body, Gwen tried to focus on that tender touch. It was so gentle, so warm; it had been so long since anyone had touched her in that way. She felt her chest rise in a deep breath, but her lungs convulsed with sudden pain. She coughed, sending agony rippling through her muscles.

"Shah." The voice was steady and calm. "It's all right. Just rest, Gwen, just rest."

That voice... it was Nick's. Was she truly dead? But hadn't she been told that there would be no pain here?

She had to know. Her eyes fluttered open, and in her blurred vision, she found his face. She was lying on something in front of him; there was a rattling noise, a sensation of movement, sunlight coming in through half-curtained windows.

"You're awake." A smile lifted the curves of Nick's face, making Gwen's heart turn over with joy.

"N-Nick?" she whispered.

"Don't try to talk," said Nick gently. "You're safe now. You're going to be all right. The doctor said it was a close thing, but he's given you medicine, and now we're going to take you to the country. Rd. Woodley will see you as soon as we get there."

Gwen stared up at him, failing to understand. The country? The doctor? Medicine? Those things were not for her; they were unattainable, belonging only to the rich.

Nick leaned forward; he was sitting on something that looked like the seat of a carriage. His fingertips trailed gently over her cheek. "Just hold on, darling," he murmured. "It's almost over. You're going to be just fine."

"Nick," she whispered again. She wanted to take his hand, but her body hurt too much. "How... how are you..." Coughs overwhelmed her, and Nick hushed her gently, wrapping his hand around hers until they were over.

"I wish you would sleep, Gwen," he said softly. "You need it."

Gwen stared up into his eyes, unable to speak, but hoping he would understand that she wanted to know what was happening. Of course he understood. He always had.

"You must have been so alone and so afraid, all these years," he murmured, stroking her hair again. "I always hoped that you and Roberta were together... until I found Bobbie two years ago. Yes," he said, smiling at the excitement in Gwen's eyes, "I found her. She's safe. She's all right – and she's going to be so happy to see you. We've been searching everywhere for you."

Gwen stared up at him, her heart thudding. Could this all be real? Was it happening?

"Bobbie thought I had died there on the wharves that night," said Nick. "I'm sure so did you. And I nearly did, too. I fell into the water with that dog, and we were struggling, and I was drowning... and then someone grabbed me, and pulled me to the surface. I wasn't breathing; he breathed for me, and took me to hospital. It was Dr. Ivor Woodley. He had been in India working at a mission station there, caring for all the poor people, and he had just gotten back from his voyage. He was walking home along the wharves when he heard the splashing and jumped into the water to save me. He told me afterwards that he never saw you or Bobbie. I know he would have saved you too."

Gwen struggled for enough breath to speak. "I led... the dogs away," she whispered. "I thought..." A tear ran down her cheek.

"Shhh. Don't be sad," said Nick. "You did everything you could. You always did, darling. We're all only alive because of you."

The words felt unreal, but she could see that he meant them.

He wiped her tears away. "Dr. Woodley took me to the hospital where he worked," he told her. "I had hypothermia, and a terrible fever besides, and he cared for me until I was well again. When I was well enough to be discharged, he knew I wouldn't survive on the streets. I was very weak; I wanted to find you and Bobbie, but I could barely walk. Dr. Woodley took me home and set me to work, first just doing little bits of work around his house, but later I learned more and more and eventually he made me his groundskeeper. And all the time, I was looking for you and Roberta." He gave a shaky smile. "I nearly gave up on finding you. But I couldn't stop looking, and once I'd found Roberta, she started looking too. The doctor moved out of London to a house in the country; Bobbie works as his cook, and your mama lives with us in a cottage on the grounds, too."

"Mama?" Gwen gasped, but she could feel her strength fading; sleep was reaching for her, whether she liked it or not.

Nick seemed to notice. He took a rug that was lying folded on the seat beside him, shook it open, and spread it over her.

"We'll see her in a little while, darling," he said. "For now, just sleep a little. We're on our way to the cottage now. When you wake up, your mama and sister will be here with you."

His voice was the last thing Gwen heard before she drifted into sleep.

~ ~ ~ ~ ~

Voices. They were all around Gwen, talking softly; she couldn't make out the words, but she knew somehow that they were good and kind. There were hands on her, too, touching her face, holding her hand. There was so much tenderness in their touch.

She was lying on something soft, and there was light on her; warmth around her. It all seemed so lovely. She wanted to experience it, and so despite the pain, she fought her way towards consciousness.

The speaking voice swam into focus. It was a masculine voice, clipped, educated, but with a current of deep warmth running through it.

"Her convalescence will take time, but the fever has broken at last," it was saying. "With fresh air and rest, I believe she will make a full recovery." It paused, deepened. "You found her just in time, Nicholas. It is pure Providence that she still lives."

"Oh, Gwen," whispered another voice – a dear, dear, wonderfully familiar voice. Roberta's voice.

Gwen had to know if she was dreaming. She opened her eyes slowly, taking in first the sunlight that flooded the bright room where she was lying, the pillows and blankets, the bed. She had never had a bed to herself before, and the glorious comfort of her limbs on the soft mattress nearly made up for the pain and weakness in her muscles. Her fingers twitched, and she heard a gasp to her left.

"Oh!" said Roberta. "I think she's waking up." There was a hand on Gwen's cheek. "Gwen, darling, can you hear me?"

With a mammoth effort, Gwen turned her head and looked at last into the blue eyes of her sister.

"Bobbie," she croaked, tears flooding her vision. "Oh, Bobbie!"

"Don't cry. Don't cry, dear, dear Gwenny," said Roberta, stroking Gwen's hair, squeezing her hand. "We're here. We're all here with you, and everything is all right. Everything is really all right at last."

Blinking away her tears, Gwen saw them gathered around her – all the people she had left to love. Nick. Roberta. Even Mama. They were all rosy-cheeked and looked so well, wearing warm clothes; Mama was sitting in a wheelchair, leaning forward, her eyes shining as they rested on Gwen in a way that she had never seen them shine before.

"Gwendoline, my dear child." Mama rested a gnarled hand on Gwen's knee.

A hand descended on Gwen's shoulder from the other side. She looked up into a lean face, with warm green eyes and a sand-coloured moustache.

"It's an Honor to finally meet you, Gwendoline," he said. "I'm Dr. Woodley, and I want you to know that you and your family will always be safe with me." He gave her shoulder a little squeeze, then withdrew.

Bewildered by happiness, Gwen stared at her family again. "How?" she gasped. "How...?"

"You've heard my part of the story," said Nick, pulling up a chair and sitting beside her, resting a hand gently on her hair. "As soon as I was settled in the cottage, with enough money, I went back to the workhouse and got your mother out of there. I was hoping she knew where you were; she had seen you a few times, but didn't know where you were staying, or where Bobbie was."

That was what the porter had meant when he had said that Mama was "gone". Tears of joy and relief trickled down Gwen's cheeks.

"Oh, I looked everywhere for you, Gwenny," said Roberta. "That night on the wharves... I woke up feeling so dizzy and confused. Nick was gone; I could hear a dog barking somewhere, but you were gone too. I was afraid of the dogs, and I ran away. I didn't know where I was going. I was just so confused and disoriented... I got completely lost in the city."

"I found her half-starved in a warehouse full of orphan thieves," said Nick. "All she wanted to do was to find you."

"We've been looking for you ever since, scouring London for you neighbourhood by neighbourhood," said Roberta. "I thought I heard your voice once, in the marketplace where Nick found you, as I was leaving in a cab. I looked back, but I didn't see you in the crowd and I'd been searching everywhere for you."

"I was there," Gwen whispered. She smiled through her tears. "It gave me such hope to see you."

"I only wish..." Tears filled Roberta's eyes. "Oh, Gwen, how you've suffered!"

"It doesn't matter now." Mama stretched out her arms, wrapping them around Roberta, Gwen, and Nick all at once. "All that matters is that we're finally together – all thanks to you, Gwen. If you hadn't kept on fighting for this family... why, we may never have survived."

Hearing those words from Mama made chains fall away from Gwen's heart. "Do you mean it?" she whispered.

"I mean it with all my heart," said Mama. "Thank you, my darling. Thank you."

Gwen leaned her head back on her pillows, feeling the arms of her loved ones around her.

Roberta had been right. Everything was really all right, at last.

Epilogue

"Joseph Robert Jones!" Gwen bellowed at the top of her voice. "Get down from there this minute!"

Joseph was hanging upside down from the topmost branches of the oak tree at the bottom of the lawn. His laughter filled the air as he swung back and forth, making Gwen's heart tremble in her chest. She marched across the grass towards him. "You're going to break your silly neck, child!" she shouted.

"Don't worry, Gwenny dear." The warm, welcome voice came from the vegetable patch. "He's just fine. He climbs like a little monkey."

Gwen looked over, a smile lifting the corners of her lips. Nick was walking towards her, dusting soil from his hands. There was dirt on his knees, but his eyes were shining with happiness and contentment. He put an arm around Gwen's shoulders and kissed her cheek, then looked up at where Joseph was swinging.

"Your mother told you to get down, young man," he said sternly.

"All right, Papa." Joseph obediently flipped the right way up and scrambled down the branches with seamless agility. Plopping to the ground, he gave Gwen a mischievous grin. He had her dark hair, but when he smiled, his brown eyes were the exact replica of her father's.

It was impossible to be angry with him for long. Especially not when he came up to her, threw his little arms around her knees, and said, "I'm sorry, Mama."

"It's all right, dear." Gwen ran a hand through his tousled hair. "Now go and wash up quickly. Your Aunt Bobbie will be here any minute now for tea."

"Hooray!" Joseph grinned. "Aunt Bobbie!"

He rushed off into the cottage, and Gwen and Nick followed a little more sedately. The evening light of summer edged everything with purest gold, and Gwen was in no hurry at all.

She looked up at Nick, so happy and strong where he walked hand-in-hand with her. "Thank you, my love," she said.

He looked down at her, surprised. "For what?" he asked.

Gwen gave a deep sight of contentment. "For everything."

They had just stepped into the cottage kitchen when there was a knock at the door. Gwen's tabby cat hurried down the hall to the door; she followed, pushing it open. Roberta was waiting on the doorstep, her blue eyes alight, and Gwen was immediately struck by how noticeable the curve of her sister's midriff had become.

"Oh, Bobbie, hello!" Gwen cried, wrapping her sister in her arms. "And hello, James!" she added over Roberta's shoulder to her young husband, who was beaming with joy and pride. It hadn't taken very long for Dr. Woodley's handsome son to fall in love with beautiful Roberta; she was an heiress now, not a cook.

Roberta laughed. "As though you didn't see us just this morning while we were walking to the bakery," she said.

"Ah, but you weren't wearing this dress then." Gwen grinned down at her, placing her hands on Roberta's swollen belly. "I can't wait to meet the little one. Have you thought of names yet?"

Roberta smiled over at her husband, taking his hand.

"We were going to go with James for a little boy," he said.

"And for a girl?" asked Gwen.

Roberta met her eyes, and there was a tiny spark of sadness in them; a memory of the suffering they had shared, yet which had only served to deepen their bond.

"Theodora Bertha," she said. "That will be her name."

"It's a perfect name." Gwen smiled, swallowing a lump in her throat. "I wish Mama could be here to meet your baby."

"At least she met yours," said Roberta, "and her last few years were filled with joy and light."

Gwen couldn't resist hugging her sister again.

"And we have so much joy and light waiting for us," she said.

Roberta smiled, the dark clouds of sorrow gone once more. "We do!" she said. "Let's go inside."

Gwen took her sister's hand. Side by side, they stepped into the cottage together.

The End

Thank you for reading my book

I hope that you enjoyed it!

Over the page you will find a preview of another of my books.

Preview

THE STONEPICKERS CHRISTMAS PROMISE

THE WAIF'S LOST FAMILY

Chapter One

Frost glittered all the way down the wharf at Canon's Marsh, making the cobbles slippery underfoot. Lilian Pearse clung to her father's calloused hand, whilst he strode with a steady, assured gait towards the *Glenelg*—a hulking, weathered ship that would soon hoist anchor and take him far away from his beloved daughter. Farther, even, than her young mind could fathom.

"Must you leave?" Lilian asked, already knowing the answer, for she had repeated the question at least a hundred times in the past month.

Her father smiled down at her. "If I could stay, you know I would."

"But... it is almost Christmas," she said feebly. "Won't there be another ship you can sail on—in the new year, perhaps?"

Regret deepened the lines of his forehead and crinkled his hooded eyes, hiding the thin, pale wrinkles that he had earned from years of squinting into the sun whilst aboard far-sailing ships. "I did my best, Lily. I tried to find a ship that didn't leave until January, but with things as they are, I can't refuse an offer when it comes along."

The landscape of Bristol's maritime trade had altered drastically in the past two decades, transforming the once-booming port, second only to London, into a waning pool of commerce. With the abolition of slavery, Bristol had lost its primary source of cargo. A just and necessary change, of course, but where other ports had immediately sought new and lucrative contracts in cotton and coal,

Bristol had suffered a drought of solutions. Unable to compete with the northern cities, not least because the heavily tidal River Avon was a treacherous route to traverse at the best of times, Bristol had been forced to take what it could get.

"I know," Lilian murmured, squeezing her father's hand. "I'm going to miss you; that's all."

"As I'll miss you," he replied, pausing on their approach to the *Glenelg*. "But think of the Christmas we'll have when I return. Doesn't matter if it's the middle of July, you and me are going to have us a Christmas celebration, and there'll be gifts for you that'll make all of Broadmead green with envy."

Lilian's heart leapt just a little, for her father never failed to bring her back the most exquisite presents. "Will you tell me stories of your voyage again?"

"I will tell you everything, my sweet girl," her father promised, scooping her up into his arms and swinging her around.

At three-and-ten years of age, Lilian supposed she was a bit too old to be whirled around by her father, but she did not care. As long as she got to hold onto him for a while longer, she would continue to ignore every last one of the disapproving stares, glaring from the eyes of the early-morning sailors and merchants and dockworkers and hawkers who scurried along the frosty wharf. Indeed, she pitied them for not having someone they loved enough to be silly with.

"Remind me of where you're headed," Lilian pleaded, though she had already memorised the route. At least, she had imagined it, for she had no real notion of where Cuba was, just that it was much too far away from Bristol for her liking.

Her father laughed and set her down. "I shall sail up the River Avon to the river mouth, where the ship will follow the coast up to South Wales. From there, we will receive our coal, which we shall take all the way to Cuba. That done, I'll be on my way home to you, laden with trinkets and tales to make up for my absence."

"Why can't Cuba mine for their own coal?" Lilian pouted a little.

"I don't think they have any," her father replied. "We're fortunate to live where we do, Lily. I know it doesn't always seem like it we're lucky souls, but there's black gold underneath England's soil, and that makes us rich indeed."

Lilian pulled a face. "Only some of us are rich."

"And, one day, when I've thought of a way to make our fortune, we will be, too," he said, with the dreamy confidence of a man who truly believed in his words. "But even if that is years from now, I promise I'll never go away for another Christmas."

She softened slightly, unable to stay cross with her father. "Swear it."

"I swear it upon my heart." He traced two lines across his chest, beaming at her as if he hoped it might coax a smile back onto her face.

Not wanting him to be sad, she gave him the smile he clearly wanted. "I will say a prayer for you every night, Papa, and pray *five* times on Christmas Day." She paused in thought. "Does it snow in Cuba?"

"I very much doubt it, so you must promise to make a snow angel for me," he replied, taking hold of her hand as they continued on down the wharf, getting ever closer to the warped and peeling exterior of the *Glenelg*.

She nodded eagerly. "I promise."

"Swear it," he parroted her with a smile.

"I swear it on Mama." She copied the motion that he had made above his heart.

Her father pulled her into a sudden, tight embrace, his rough hand gently stroking her wispy, blonde hair. "She is watching over the both of us, always. It'll be her guidance and your prayers that see me home safely, and I'm already looking forward to it." He sighed. "Nothing warms my heart more than when the ship is coming into shore, and I see you standing there, waiting. I still don't know how you always get the time right."

"It's a mystery I'm not prepared to share," Lilian teased, though it was actually rather simple.

She had a friend at the docks—a grizzled, wise old man by the name of Timothy Plockton—who had a keen knowledge of what the tide would bring. He knew the name of every ship that went out and every ship that came in and could guess, with astonishing accuracy, when the ships would return.

All she had to do was ask Timothy when her father's ship was due, and he would give her his best guess. On that day, she would wait, come rain or shine, and Timothy had not been wrong yet.

"There's a part of me that doesn't want to know. I like the magic of it," her father said, slowly releasing her.

She tried to cling on, realising that the moment of departure was sweeping towards her at a swift and saddening pace.

Her father had been a sailor for as long as she could remember, but it never got any easier to say farewell. Three years ago, she had, at least, had her mother's company to keep her warm and safe through the lengthy absences, both of them growing giddier as her father's return date had come closer. But, no more. Now, her father's return was the *only* thing she had to look forward to, and every departure was harder to bear because of it.

"I have to go now, my girl," her father said softly, half-turning toward the *Glenelg's* gangway.

Above, sailors hurried back and forth behind the bulwark, readying the vessel for embarkation. It would be some time before the ship actually sailed away from the wharf, which was often the most difficult part for Lilian—to watch from land, wishing her father could stay, wishing he would just stride back down the gangway towards her, yet knowing he would not.

"I love you," Lilian whispered, gripping fistfuls of his shirt sleeves, not ready to bid him farewell.

He smiled one of his warmest smiles; the kind that made his blue eyes twinkle. "I love you more, little egg. I'll be back before you know it."

"You had better be, or I shall be very cross indeed," she told him, trying to hide her welling tears behind a brave smile.

She had always loved his nickname for her, 'little egg,' though he did not use it as often these days.

According to him, it had begun when she was born, and her bald, baby head had reminded him of a little egg. And though she was growing older, which was likely why he did not use it much.

It cheered her heart whenever he called her that, reminding her of a thousand joyful, childhood memories: summer days at nearby Clevedon, playing on the beach with her mother and father; long autumn walks on the Downs; eating hot, buttered toast in the dead of winter with snow falling outside, and the Christmases they used to share, muddling together a feast from whatever they could get and sharing their humble harvest with anyone who needed feeding.

The stories and the merriment of those bygone Christmases would always be a blessed memory, their magic never to be repeated.

With one last, fierce embrace, Lilian's father carefully pried her off him, placed a sweet kiss upon her brow, and headed up the gangway to join his fellow sailors. He looked back the entire time, until his work swallowed him up. Nevertheless, Lilian knew he would reappear when the ship began to pull away, offering one final wave and keeping his eye upon her until distance parted them again.

He will be home before I know it, Lilian told herself, as she pulled her cloak tighter around her thin body and tried not to shiver. Her gaze turned up towards the sky, where bruised clouds of brownish-grey scudded slowly over the city, promising the very snow that she had vowed to make an angel in.

She allowed herself a hopeful smile, thinking of all the Christmases yet to come, and the snowmen and snow angels she would make with her father, and the feasts that they would share together.

Perhaps, when he returned from this voyage, he would have made enough coin for them to move out of the lodgings they shared with her aunt and uncle. Perhaps, they would even be able to rent the old terrace where they used to live, when Lilian's mother was still alive. *That*, to Lilian, would have been a true Christmas miracle.

Just then, the ship began to pull away from the wharf, belching blackened smoke.

Lilian willed it to falter, urged it to sit still in the water, unable to undertake its lengthy voyage. A foolish wish, of course, but her young heart could not help it.

As the ship turned, heading up to the curve that would lead it through Bathurst Basin and into the proper tides and tribulations of the River Avon, a figure appeared at the stern. Lilian's father clambered up as high as he could and raised his hand in a vigorous wave, his mouth stretched into the widest smile.

Heart breaking, Lilian raised her hand in return, waving until she thought her arm might drop off as she ran alongside the departing vessel.

It was their tradition, and though her lungs hurt from the cold, winter air being sucked down into them, and her stiff legs burned from the exertion, she hurried on until the land cut her off.

There, unable to go any further, she stood, heaving out great breaths as she continued to wave with all her might, hoping that her determination would deliver her message across the water: *I love you, Papa. I love you. Be safe and come home quickly.*

Wind whipped up around her and whistled outward, as if it meant to take her message to her father personally. He still stood on the bow, waving his arm slowly, giving Lilian all the time she needed to hold his image in her memory. And when he came back, many months from now, his painstaking approach would be even more frustrating than his sluggish departure.

Struck by a sudden thought, Lilian cupped her hands around her mouth and shouted, as loudly as she could, "Merry Christmas, Papa!"

Her father halted his wave for a moment, and though he was disappearing further and further into the distance, Lilian knew she heard his faint reply. "Merry Christmas, little egg!"

No fire could have kept her warmer than those words, and even though he would not be with her when Christmas *did* come, she would hold his festive wishes dear to her heart. A gift that could not be taken away from her, no matter how hard her aunt tried.

Chapter Two

"Gracious me, girl, what are you doin'?" Josephine Cross barked, looming over the threadbare, soot-stained blanket that served as Lilian's bed. Only when her father was gone, of course.

Lilian stirred, eking open tired eyes that felt swollen from the cold of the lodgings. "Hmm?"

"Get up, you wretched girl!" Josephine grabbed Lilian by the wrist and hauled her up with a savagery that sent a jarring pain up Lilian's arm. "Your father isn't here now, girl. You don't get to loaf around as you please."

Lilian fumbled for a reply, but words would not come. Her mouth was numb, her jaw locked from a night of shivering.

The corner where she slept had cracks in the wall, allowing the icy tongues of a draught inside, and Lilian's thin blanket could do nothing to keep the chill at bay.

"Are you just goin' to stare at me like a dolt?" Josephine hissed, shaking Lilian's arm. "Get yourself dressed and get to work, you lazy beast!"

For a few moments, Lilian continued to blink in confusion, for she had been deep in a dangerous slumber that was proving hard to fully awaken from. It was the same sort of sleep that carried souls away from bitter streets and frosted doorways every night in the wintertime.

In a way, Lilian felt somewhat grateful for her aunt's vicious method of awakening, for if Josephine had *not* shaken her awake, she wondered if she would have awoken at all.

"Is... there breakfast?" Lilian managed to say, moving her jaw to try and urge some life back into it.

Josephine scoffed as if Lilian had just asked for the crown jewels. "You get breakfast when you earn your keep, girl. Now, do as I've asked and get out of my sight. There are scraps to be picked, and they won't pick 'emselves."

It would not be the first morning that Lilian went without so much as a morsel to eat, though she had grown accustomed to not starving whilst her father had been at home.

Her aunt and uncle never said a harsh word or denied her anything while she had her father's protection, but the safety of him had sailed away three days ago.

With him, too, the security of knowing where her next meal would come from, and whether or not she would open her eyes in the morning or freeze to death in the night.

"You are supposed to take care of me," Lilian said quietly, her eyes filling with tears. "Papa gives you coin for my keep."

Josephine scoffed. "What my brother gives me for your "keep" wouldn't be enough to feed a sparrow for a day. As if I don't have enough mouths to feed, without you trying to steal the scraps right out from under my own wains." She jabbed a finger toward the door of the lodgings. "You don't see them loafin' around, doin' nothin'. They're all out, doin' their day's work. You're the only one thinkin' 'emselves too high and mighty. Well, your father isn't here to spoil you no more."

Lilian's five cousins were as foul as their mother and father.

The four boys were older, between four-and-ten and nine-and-ten, while Josephine's only daughter, Marie, was twelve years of age. *She* was not expected to scour the streets, gathering scraps and trying to sell them for anything anyone would offer. Indeed, Marie was the very epitome of a spoiled little girl, lounging in front of the fireplace all day, claiming she was "too poorly" to lift a finger.

As a child, she had almost died of a terrible grippe, and had milked that bygone ailment ever since, though she was in ruder health than any of the family.

"Yes, it really is a disgrace that you've been sleeping for so long. I'm awake, even though my chest is very sore today," Marie chimed in, at that moment, from her cot by the fireplace.

She lay on her side, reclined, chewing loudly upon two slices of thick bread, drenched in dripping. The scent made Lilian's dry mouth water.

Josephine made a soft, cooing sound. "Don't vex yourself, sweet Marie. You know it does you no good." She whirled around, glaring at Lilian.

"See what you've done? If my girl falls sick again, because of you, I won't hesitate to kick you out on your arse."

She's not even sick, and it's my papa's coin that you use to pay for the lie, Lilian held her tongue, knowing it was a battle she could not win.

Josephine would not listen to anyone who said her daughter was in fine health, to the point where she frequently wasted a small fortune on tinctures and tonics from the apothecary.

Lilian was convinced that the apothecary just put cheap oil in a vial and charged whatever he liked, for even he must have known that there was nothing wrong with Marie.

"I'll be on my way," Lilian said quietly, gathering up her garments and taking them into the small, square room—barely more than a cupboard—that belonged to her father.

When he was at home, she slept on a cot in that room. When he was at sea, she was forbidden from sleeping in there, for her eldest cousin, David, used it for himself.

She was not permitted to tell her father that David slept in there, just as she was not permitted to breathe a word of the cruelty she faced when her father was gone. Indeed, Lilian was threatened most viciously, told that she would be left out in the cold or handed in to the workhouse if she dared to say anything.

"I miss you, Papa," Lilian whispered, as she quickly donned her thick, woollen dress: a garment her father had purchased for the brutal winter months, though she guessed it would not be long before it suddenly "disappeared."

Most of her belongings had a habit of vanishing in her father's absence, and though she knew her aunt had stolen the items in order to sell them for more useless medicines, Lilian could not complain. Nor did she ever have evidence.

The only things that Lilian ever managed to save were the trinkets and gifts that her father brought her after every voyage, for she had a hiding place that no one, not even her father, knew about.

She glanced at the corner of the room, eyeing a particular brick at the very bottom of the wall.

She squinted to get a better look, making sure no brick dust had tumbled down onto the floor—a tell-tale sign that someone had tampered with the hiding place. To her relief, all seemed intact and just how she had left it when she was forced out into the main room.

"I swear, if you make me tell you again, you'll go the whole week without a meal in you!" Josephine bellowed from outside the bedroom door, making Lilian jump in fright.

"I'm done, Aunt Josephine!" Lilian replied hurriedly, throwing on her cloak and fastening the laces on her new boots, before heading out.

She was halfway to the front door, when Josephine grabbed her by the shoulder and spun her around.

"What are those?" Josephine hissed.

Lilian frowned. "What, Aunt Josephine?"

"What are those, on your feet?"

"Boots, Aunt Josephine."

"And where did you get such boots, when my darlin' Marie's boots are fallin' to pieces?"

Lilian swallowed uncomfortably. "I've been wearing them for weeks, Aunt Josephine. Papa bought them for me, so I wouldn't be cold."

"Take them off," Josephine ordered, in a quiet, menacing voice. "You can make do with Marie's."

Lilian's eyes widened in desperation. "But, Marie has smaller feet than I do. These will be much too big for her."

"Take them off!" Josephine's command became a howl, and if Lilian continued to resist, that howl would become a scream that brought the neighbours running.

Lilian had witnessed it before, when she had refused to give up her cloak the previous winter, and she had still had it taken away from her. Now, it was likely upon the shoulders of some stevedore's wife who still could not believe the bargain she had received.

Josephine might have sold everything she could get her hands on, but she was terrible at fetching a good price.

Bending double, Lilian did as she was told, biting back angry tears as she unlaced the precious, freshly polished black boots and handed them over. A holey, dilapidated pair of brown boots, the toes gaping like mocking mouths where the leather had come apart from the soles, were thrown at Lilian's feet as replacements. She knew that Marie had not worn those particular boots for at least two years, and braced for the pinching pain of such ill-fitting shoes. Indeed, it made the prospect of wandering the city all day, searching for scraps, all the more dreadful.

Perhaps, the gaping toes would prove to be a blessing... if she had just had socks to keep some of the cold out.

"Would you take the cloak off my back, too?" Lilian muttered, struggling to control her ire.

Josephine snorted. "If you're not careful and you don't watch your mouth, then aye, I will."

Keeping her head down, certain her cheeks must be a flaming red, Lilian scooped up the broken basket by the door and headed out of the four-room lodgings that she hated to call "home."

The moment she stepped out onto the cobbled street, an icy wind nipped at her face like a secondary scolding, as if to say, *"It's your own fault for not telling your papa the truth."* In a way, that knowledge hurt more than the vicious pinch of her boots and the bitter breath of the winter gusts or any tongue-lashing her aunt could give her.

There had been countless opportunities for her to speak up when her father was there, but she remained petrified of opening her mouth and saying too much. Every time she had almost explained her suffering to him, her throat constricted, choking her back into silence.

She drew her cloak tighter around her aching body, tucked her chin into the woollen collar, and hurried away from the grimy terrace. All the while, under her breath, she repeated four words, "I miss you, Papa. I miss you, Papa. I miss you, Papa."

Maybe, she thought her small prayer would be able to reach him, half a world away, if she just whispered it often enough. Still, nothing but time could bring him back to her, and it seemed to be ticking far slower than usual.

READ THE REST

List of Books

The Pickpocket Orphans

The Workhouse Girls Despair

The Forgotten Match Girl's Christmas Birthday

The Wretched Needle Worker

The Lost Daughter

The Christmas Pauper

Printed in Great Britain
by Amazon